Escape of the Duke
Escape, Book 4
Mary Lancaster

Escape of the Duke

Chapter One

H is current grace of Isbourne, Rudolph John De'Ath, had always been known to those with a dark turn of humour as the Duke of Death. This posthumous child of the sixth duke had not been expected to live more than a few hours, and ever since his birth, day by day, year by year, everyone he knew appeared to be waiting anxiously for him to die.

That he had survived infancy, despite so many illnesses, had amazed his relatives, guardians, and physicians. Despite several more maladies, no one was as surprised as the young duke himself to attain his majority in the spring of 1811. Over a year later, at the ripe old age of two-and-twenty, during a family conference at his main seat of Isley Place, he realized that the uncles seemed to have finally struggled out of their pessimism.

"The dukedom," Uncle Hazlett pronounced, "endures. We must proceed to the next step."

His grace was heartily glad to hear it. Recently, he had come to regard himself in terms of a barrel of gunpowder with the fuse rope burning ever closer, and at Lord Hazlett's unprecedented optimism, the burning slowed and sputtered into hope.

Uncle Deptford nodded wisely. "It is time, my boy."

The duke, who had been standing by the sunny window, gazing over his lush acres so that his face would not give away his internal explosions, turned to give his uncles his full and eager attention.

"You mean to break the Trust early?" he asked, almost afraid to breath.

By the terms of his father's will, the uncles and family solicitors were the trustees of his person and his estate until he was five-and-twenty, unless he married, or they agreed unanimously to hand the reins over earlier.

"An inevitable outcome," Uncle Lacey said.

At last. The duke walked across to the table and sat down. "I am ready for the responsibility. Over the last few years, I have spent much time with Gatting on the management of the estate. I have been reading on the subject too, and we have been discussing ideas for the future. I am sure that between us—"

"Oh, no, my boy!" Uncle Hazlett sounded scandalized. "There is no need for you to tire yourself, let alone dirty your hands over that sort of thing. Gatting will continue to do his duty well under our own exacting eyes. The truth is, Isbourne, the dukedom needs heirs. You must marry and fill the Isbourne nursery—"

He broke off rather suddenly, leaving the words *"before it is too late"* unsaid but somehow hanging loudly in the air. The disaster of the dukedom reverting to the Crown had been held over the duke all his life. He had grown up with the weight of that responsibility, the knowledge that it was his duty to take care of himself and survive as long as he could for the sake of all the people and the land that depended upon him, for all the great history of his ancestors. His frail, sickly person was all that stood in the way of catastrophe.

It was an intolerably dull life, just surviving. In the last year or so, since coming down from Oxford, his interest in his acres and his tenants and workers was all that he had. Fortunately, the subject fascinated him, and he was eager to take up the reins and, with Gatting the steward's help, to make ambitious improvements.

It took a moment for Uncle Hazlett's words to penetrate. The subject had been changed.

The duke closed his mouth. "Nursery," he repeated blankly. "Marriage." *But* I *have not even lived...*

"That's the ticket," Uncle Lacey said, beaming at him.

"And the perfect lady is available," Uncle Hazlett told him. He might have been recommending a horse.

"She is?" Isbourne was torn between astonishment and outrage. *Even in this...*

Hazlett nodded. "It was an arrangement agreed by his grace your father with the Earl of Sark. That the eldest Isbourne son should ally with a Sark daughter. And Lady Lily is now eighteen years old. Your father and the late Lord Sark were great friends, of course, but the new earl is quite amenable to the match."

"Is he." The duke's words did not quite constitute a question, more of a blank statement.

The uncles did not notice.

"Oh yes," Hazlett said. "In fact, he is anxious to detach her from her stepmother's unsuitable care and influence.

"And the young lady concerned?" Isbourne asked.

"Oh, Lady Lily is an old friend of *yours*," Uncle Deptford said.

Isbourne blinked, for he did not have any friends. "She is?"

"You met as children, here at Isley Place."

Isbourne's encounters with other children were not so many that he could have forgotten. He had a vague recollection of a pretty little girl in pigtails hiding behind her mother's skirts until the two of them were hailed off to the nursery by both of their nurses. He had been ten years old. Lily was a mere six, and Isbourne had found her half-fascinating—for she was another child—and half-silly, for she was interested in bizarre things like tiny tea-cups and dolls and his old carved dog on wheels that he hadn't touched for years. She had mostly played on her own while he had read his book, until the little girl's nurse offered to take them both to play by the lake.

Nurse Blossom, his own nurse, had refused to allow it, so the little girl had gone without him, while Isbourne had watched enviously from the window as the child ran and skipped and picked flowers into the distance.

It was one of the only two childhood occasions on which he had met anyone of roughly his own age and rank. On the second, he must have been fourteen or so when the uncles had brought the Earl of Sanderly's two sons for a short visit. Since the other boys had been eighteen and twenty respectively, they weren't terribly interested in a sickly adolescent, and he had felt somewhat overwhelmed by their size and energy and the fact that the younger already had an army commission and was heading off to war. They had been carelessly kind to him, taken him for a short ramble with them and he had tried to keep up. It was his tutor who put a stop to that, insisting it was far too tiring for him to go any further. He had even, humiliatingly, been sent to bed to rest.

Tragically enough, it had been the elder of those two terrifyingly healthy boys who had died, making the younger the new earl. And Isbourne, doggedly defeating the wagerers and the worst fears of his uncles, guardians, doctors, nurses, and tutors, who was still clinging onto life. Though God knew why.

"You want me to marry Lily Lisle," Isbourne said with deliberation. "When?"

"Oh, the sooner the better, we think."

Do you? "What does Lily think?"

Uncle Hazlett blinked. "She is an agreeable girl, sweet-natured, dutiful, and submissive. Of course she is happy to marry you. She will be a duchess. Her son will be Duke of Isbourne one day."

"I would like to see her before we agree to this."

All three uncles gaped at him. This was only the second time he had ever argued with them. The first had been about going to Oxford. He had won that one although the subsequent experience had been somewhat...disappointing. Not to say humiliating.

"Well," Uncle Deptford said dubiously. "It is only right that we should arrange a meeting. I shall ask Lady Sark to bring her here for a night or two. Perhaps next week."

For no obvious reason, the little victory did not please the duke. He envisioned a slightly more adult version of their previous meeting, constrained and chaperoned, where he could never establish what she wanted, let alone what he did.

No, that was not true. He was not ready to wed anyone. Marriage would not give him the freedom he craved like a starving man. It would only substitute one lot of fetters for another while the powder keg continued to burn.

In fact, if anything, the idea of being chained to a silly girl for the sole purpose of begetting children, appalled him. He could not marry her at all unless he knew the girl was willing to be sacrificed, and who would truly choose to be chained to an invalid until he had the good manners to turn up his toes? Leaving a nursery full of boys behind him, of course.

It all felt so bizarre that he didn't know whether to laugh or run screaming from the room until they sent for the doctor. Which would not be hard since the man still lived in the house.

As he gazed from one uncle to the next, he thought longingly of his old boyhood fantasy of escaping the lot of them, of ignoring the hurt and the panic that he would leave behind him, shrugging off all he owed to them and to his name, just to go somewhere else, *anywhere* else, blissfully alone...

This vision had got him to Oxford, though *not* alone. In order to achieve his goal, he had made so many concessions that he might as well have stayed at home, despite the first- class degree he had attained. He had been seventeen then. Now he was two-and-twenty and surely anything was possible. And he needn't do it by quarrelling.

"I have a better idea," he said, as the sudden excitement caught him by the throat. "I shall call on Lady Lily on my own, and she and I will decide if we should suit, and when."

The uncles exchanged glances, but they had never been cruel. By their own lights, they had devoted themselves selflessly to his person and his interests. They must have recognized that the wedding—to say nothing of the begetting of children—would be a far quicker and less fraught affair if he and Lily liked each other.

"We could possibly arrange for that," Uncle Hazlett said cautiously at last.

"No, I shall do it myself, Uncle," Isbourne said, springing to his feet. "As you say, it is time."

They could see the sense in that too. In fact, after his original reaction, they were probably relieved to have won him over so easily with such a minor concession. They probably imagined that an uncle and a doctor could easily be added to his entourage when he departed. What they did not grasp until later was that he did not say *when* he would arrange to call on Lady Lily.

In fact, he slipped away from Isley Place that very night, leaving a gracious note to Lord Hazlett to explain that he was going away for a month or two, during which time he would most certainly call on Lady Lily. There was another note for his kind old valet, and for his groom who had taught him to ride very carefully the gentlest of well-mannered horses.

Saddling, bridling, and grooming, were, of course, the safer lessons in horsemanship, and Isbourne was particularly skilled in them, so he had no trouble at all in preparing his own mount and riding quietly off into the night.

A massive relief, a sense of freedom that was almost joy began to build up inside him as he approached his own lantern-lit gates. The land beyond was still his, of course, but it was the open road, and he took it with huge excitement, in search of his first, long-awaited adventure.

He was no longer the Duke of Isbourne. To himself and everyone else he encountered, he would be merely Jack, which had been the name of his remote childhood before everyone had addressed him only by his title, as if he existed in no other form and with no other meaning.

Well, Jack was back, and he intended to have fun.

SOME THREE WEEKS LATER, he was seriously discommoded for the first time. He stood by the side of the road watching a plausible ruffian ride off at the gallop, taking his horse, his pistol, and all the cash in his pocket.

Jack did not much care for the highwayman who had robbed him, but it was certainly another experience to add to his growing list. Plus, it was a long walk to the next town, and he wasn't convinced he could achieve it before nightfall. A glance at the darkening sky warned him that rain was on the way.

Shrugging philosophically, he strode out, feeling slightly bereft without his horse. Not that it was his own nag. He had changed horses frequently on his erratic journey—almost as often as he changed his surname—so that he would be harder to trace. But he had developed some kind of friendship with each of those equines, the difficult and the obedient, the tired and the frisky. He had met a number of interesting people, too, many of whom he had liked a great deal, and would never have encountered in the normal course of his life.

The highwayman was not one of those.

He had only been walking for about a quarter of an hour when a travelling coach pulled by four matching chestnuts swept past him in a cloud of dust. There were two coachmen on the box, and two outriders bristling with weapons.

To his surprise, this impressive equipage slowed and moved further to the side of the road where it halted. One of the outriders and a coachman seemed to be having a conference through the coach window with their passengers.

Rather wiser than before his trip began, the duke approached with caution. The outrider appeared to be waiting civilly for him, but despite the outward respectability, he knew there were many tricks and flim-flams to be played on the unsuspecting. The outrider turned his mount to face Jack and tugged his hat.

"Sir, my mistress is concerned that you were held up on the road."

Jack halted some feet from him and rather wished the highwayman had not taken his pistol. "What could have made her imagine such a thing?"

Before the outrider could answer, the coach door sprang open and a lady's head appeared. It was an undeniably beautiful head of copper-red curls framing a face so lovely that he forgot to breathe. Large, hazel-green eyes, exquisite cheek bones, full-lipped, almost sulky mouth.

Languidly, she looked him up and down.

"It may," she drawled in a low, charmingly husky voice, "have something to do with the fact that you are in riding dress without a horse, coupled with our own recent experience seeing off a ruffian with *two* horses, who tried to hold us up too."

Isbourne bowed. "Then I congratulate you, ma'am. I confess I came off rather worse."

"Well, we shall both have our revenge by reporting the villain at the next town. Did he take everything?"

Isbourne turned out his pockets out to show the linings. Not even a penny remained there.

"Dear me. May I offer you a seat in my carriage, since we appear to be traveling in the same direction?"

Isbourne regarded her lovely yet weary young face, the elegant hat adorning her perfectly coiffed auburn curls and knew there were several tricks of this order. And he had already proved himself to be an easy mark. Against this, he weighed up his empty pockets, her polite ennui, her fascinating eyes, veiled in feminine mystery yet frankly amused at his caution. He also took into consideration the clear disapproval of her scowling servants. And his own inclinations. To say nothing of the rain clouds above which threatened a severe soaking.

"If it would not be an imposition," he said diffidently, "I should be very grateful to be taken as far as Cogglesworth."

The lady inclined her head and vanished from his view.

"Mind how you go, sir," the coachman said pleasantly, yet with a clear warning in his voice as Jack climbed into the carriage and sat down in the vacant seat with his back to the horses.

The lady sat opposite him, alone, without maid or chaperone. Her servant's warning to him began to make more sense. Jack might have had no experience of Society, but he knew the rules of propriety and etiquette.

The coach began to rumble forward, while she eyed him with an expression he could not read.

He said seriously, "This is indeed an imposition. I beg your pardon. I had not realized you were alone. You will not like to be seen with me in a closed carriage."

A gleam of mockery eased into her eyes. "My dear sir, I am a widow, not a debutante, and there is much worse gossip to my name. It is *your* reputation that is liable to suffer."

"Well, I shan't tell if you don't."

That surprised a quick breath that might have been laughter. She settled back gracefully against the velvet squabs, watching him. "It strikes me, that for such a young man, you are taking your highway robbery very much in your stride."

"Well, I have never been robbed before, so the mechanics of it were interesting, if quite inconvenient until you took me up."

"I'm afraid there will be further inconveniences at Cogglesworth. I hope you have friends there?"

"Oh, no," he said vaguely. "I will merely be passing through."

"How?" she said at once. "You can have no means of buying another horse or paying your shot at the inn for the night. Yet you maintain a rather astonishing...insouciance."

"Not quite so astonishing," Jack said, crossing his left calf across his right knee and poking his fingers inside his mud-stained boot, while the lady watched him with some fascination.

When he fished out the roll of banknotes that had been wrapped around his leg, she laughed with genuine amusement that brought an involuntary smile to his own lips.

"Why, you are rather more than a pretty face," she drawled. "I suppose you have a pistol in the other boot?"

"Sadly not. It made walking too hazardous. Perhaps you would tell me to whom I am indebted for my rescue?"

"Then you did not see the crest on the carriage door?"

"I had other things on my mind, although a crest does impress. My name is Jack De'Ath." He used the name only very occasionally, but for some reason he wanted to give his rescuer the version nearest the truth.

Her eyebrows rose. "Not one of the Isbourne De'Aths? I didn't know there were any left. Apart from the duke."

"The Duke of Death?" Jack said boldly. "He certainly doesn't acknowledge the connection. If he is still alive."

"Oh, he is," the lady said unexpectedly, preventing him from changing the subject as he intended. "Or at least he was a year or so ago. My brother knew him at Oxford."

The duke blinked. He hadn't known anyone at Oxford apart from the tutors and doctors and chaplains who had travelled with him, plus a college professor or two. And Amy who had cleaned his rooms.

"Well," the lady continued, as though she perceived his scepticism, "perhaps *saw* him at Oxford would be more accurate. Barty glimpsed him occasionally surrounded by his entourage, poor boy, but never spoke to him. No one did."

Poor boy. The description set his teeth on edge for some reason. There were times he had felt sorry for himself, but other people's pity was intolerable. Particularly hers.

She said, "There was an *on dit* in London in the spring that his grace was dead—"

"At last," Isbourne interpolated.

"As you say. And that the family were keeping it quiet so that the estate could be maintained and all the pensions paid as before."

"Amusing," Jack said.

"Do you think so?"

Was that disappointment in her languid voice? At any rate, there was silence until she spoke again.

"Are you travelling far, Mr. De'Ath?"

Relieved by the change of subject and wishing he had used a different surname after all, Jack said vaguely, "I have not decided."

She blinked. "You have no destination in mind?"

"I do," he admitted. "I'm just not sure how long I should take to get there."

Again, amusement sparked through the weariness in her eyes. "So you just go where the spirit takes you? Good for you. One should not be wedded to custom—London for the Season, Brighton for summer, visiting friends and relatives in the autumn—and yet so many of us do it."

"Why?" he asked.

She shrugged. "Habit, boredom, company. And occasionally, the unavoidable responsibility—you are lucky if you have none of those."

"I am escaping them, temporarily. I should probably go home soon." Or at least write to the uncles to prevent any hue and cry for him, or even a repeat of the rumours of his death that the lady had mentioned. He stirred and met her gaze so suddenly that he surprised a warm, wistful expression on her face. His heart gave a funny little bound because she was looking at him, though he suspected she did not actually see him, just her own private thoughts.

"You never did tell me your name," he remarked.

She sat forward a little, extending one languid, gloved hand. "Tabitha Lisle. Such a good name for a widow, is it not? Old and fluffy like everyone's favourite great aunt. Or cat."

Hastily, he took her slender fingers and nodded over them which was as much courtesy as one could manage while seated in a coach. He hoped it covered his unease, for Lisle was the family name of the Earl of Sark and therefore of the woman he was expected to marry. And it could be no co-incidence that they were travelling in the vague direction of the earl's country seat.

Perhaps Tabitha was the widow of one of old Sark's sons. It was amazing how many people seemed to have died before Jack.

An even more alarming thought struck him. Could this be *Lily*, up to mischief and giving a name as misleading as his own? He could see no discernible likeness to the child he had met, but it had been a long time ago and his own memory was likely to be clouded.

This woman, Tabitha, was young but not girlish. He did not feel competent to guess her age, but surely an unmarried girl of such rank would not be travelling unchaperoned? No, she must be the widow she claimed to be.

He must have stared too long, for a tired, cynical smile curled her lips. "Yes, I am *that* Lisle, the Damned Dowager of Sark, the Wicked Widow herself. But you may safely release my hand. I shan't use it to importune or seduce."

He let her go at once, but he was not shocked by her blatant little speech, as she clearly intended him to be. There was too much challenge in it.

"Why do people call you those things?" he asked.

Again, he seemed to surprise her. "Because they are true. In my defence, they called Sark the Damned Earl, didn't they? But the Wicked Widow is all my own work."

"And are you?"

"Wicked?" she said. "When I choose to be. What of you?"

"Oh," he said vaguely, "one cannot be good all of the time."

She laughed, her eyes flashing with something unreadable and yet unbearably exciting. "A man after my own heart."

Chapter Two

Tabitha was intrigued. The pale and fragile gentleman she had taken pity on was curiously ageless. Although he possessed the poise of a much older man, the lines of pain and suffering seemed etched into a much younger face. There was something at once frail and strong about him that she had never come across before, and it did not hurt that he was tall-ish and handsome in a fine-boned, almost breakable kind of a way. And his deep, soft voice seemed to do something very strange and *melty* to her bones.

When she had glimpsed him from the carriage window, he had been striding out with grace and a sort of indefatigable sense of freedom that attracted her at once. He had proved to be good mannered and shy, and remarkably un-disgruntled by his misfortune. Not quite like anyone else she had ever met. He said odd things, humorous things with a straight face. Always attracted by novelty, she had also rather liked the diffident admiration she read in his eyes, until he had gazed at her with such speculation when she mentioned the name Lisle.

Disappointment that he was not different after all was unexpectedly intense. And yet he did not appear remotely shocked, only surprised, as if he had never heard of her reputation and didn't much care anyway.

He was, she reflected, a mysterious youth, drifting alone about the countryside. It did cross her mind that he was evading the law—but she had heard of no recent duels save Lord Durward's latest, and this Mr. De'Ath seemed far too educated and civilized for other forms of crime.

When she lapsed into silence, so did he, almost as though he respected her right not to make conversation if she chose. In fact, he seemed perfectly comfortable with it. Watching him surreptitiously, she almost wished they had not told each other their names, so that they could remain strangers, attracted to each other, and able to act on that attraction or not without embarrassment or repercussions.

She wondered again how old he was, though it scarcely mattered. With that face and that poise, he would have some experience of women. Her gaze rested on his thin, long lips, firm and yet gentle in repose. She wondered how he would kiss, and then, more shockingly, what kind of a lover he would be...

Hastily, she looked away. This was no time—or place—for dalliance. After all, she was too close to home, where she meant to collect Lily and take her to Louisa Hawthorn's gathering.

She cast him another speculative glance. "I suppose you are going to Lady Hawthorne's party?"

"I am not acquainted with Lady Hawthorn. Is that your destination?"

"When my baggage and my maid catch up with me and I have collected my stepdaughter."

Something changed in his eyes, though she could not quite read it. "Are you a wicked stepmother too?"

"So Sark tells me, but my husband willed her care to me until she marries."

"Is that occasion imminent?" he asked.

"Not if I have any say in the matter—and I do. Eighteen is too young to be married."

An odd look came into his eyes. "And yet many people are."

"Including me," she said with deliberate lightness.

His perceptive gaze was suddenly unbearable, and she looked away. The thought of her late husband still made her shudder. At least she now had the power to prevent a similar disaster for Lily.

"How long have you been widowed?" he asked.

"Two years and three months. Too late for condolences." It had always been too late for those. "What will you do in Cogglesworth?"

She risked a glance at him and his serious expression relaxed into surely the sweetest smile she had ever seen on a man.

"I hope to dine with you."

Her eyebrows flew up. What shocked her was not that he had asked, but that she was so tempted to accept. Even as she knew she could not.

Perhaps he read the conflict in her face, for he said gravely, "I shan't use the occasion to importune or seduce."

Laughter took her by surprise, because he had used her own words back at her. But she met his gaze like a challenge. "Then it is as well that I have bespoken the inn's one private parlour, is it not?"

THEY ARRIVED IN COGGLESWORTH late in the afternoon, and on the innkeeper's directions, Mr. De'Ath went off immediately to buy a new horse.

Foolishly, perhaps, Tabitha looked forward to her quiet supper with him. Despite her previous experiences with the male of the species, she tended to believe his declaration of gentlemanly conduct, and while part of her might have been piqued, the more important, thinking parts, liked the absence of all that silliness. She wanted to know him better.

The George was not a posting house, but a quiet, almost rural inn on the edge of the town, where she was known. It was usually her last stopping place before Sark Park. She did not even have to worry about her dress, for she carried with her only an overnight bag. He would have to put up with her in her travelling gown, which was admittedly fashionable as well as becoming.

Laughing at herself, she went down to her private parlour, where the table was already set, and was brought a glass of sherry by the innkeeper's wife.

As she sipped it, it struck her suddenly that Mr. De'Ath might simply gallop off on his new horse, with or without apology. That would be...disappointing.

But it seemed he had not. The innkeeper showed him into the room only a minute later and poured him a glass of sherry too.

Again, she was struck by the extraordinary fragility of his appearance. There seemed to be not an ounce of fat on his body and the pale skin of his face stretched taut over the fine bones. Yet there was nothing languid about him. Every movement had an air of suppressed energy; his whole face was alive with interest, curiosity, and sheer vitality that fascinated her. Had she *ever* been so enthused for life?

Once, perhaps, before she met it head-on in marriage.

"Well?" she asked languidly, as he sat opposite her by the empty fireplace. "Did you locate a suitable horse?"

"I did. A friendly creature."

"Friendly?" she repeated. "Was that your chief requirement?"

His smile was endearingly sheepish. "Yes."

"Most gentlemen will choose something showy, or a beast with proven stamina or particular bloodlines."

"I require none of those."

"Then you don't hunt?"

"No." Was that a trace of regret? "Do you?"

"I have done. I enjoyed the danger."

A hint of something very like longing sparked in his eyes before they focused on her. "Why?"

It was so totally unexpected that she almost panicked to find an answer. She waved one languid arm. "Oh, just to relieve the monotony, you know. Life in the country can be confoundedly dull."

"That is true," he said with unexpected fervour.

"Yet you do not strike me as much of a Town man."

"I'm sure I don't. Which is your preference?"

She sipped her sherry and considered. "I believe I like to keep moving."

He smiled as though he agreed. He had a singularly sweet smile, at once boyish and appreciative, quite without malice.

"Tell me about your life, Mr. De'Ath," she said lightly. "Do you have an occupation, or do you ride your ancestral acres at leisure?"

"I have been known to ride my acres," he said. "But my life has been extraordinarily dull. I would rather learn about yours. Did you like being married?"

"No," she said before she realized that both the question and the answer were outrageous.

"Because you were only eighteen?"

"The fault was naturally mine," she said cynically.

"Do you have children?"

"No." Perhaps that would have made it all more bearable. "But I have several stepdaughters, all but one of them married with children of their own. Which makes me a grandmother, so they tell me."

His gaze was uncomfortably penetrating, so she was quite glad that the inn servants bustled in with their meal. With perfect courtesy, Mr. De'Ath conducted her to the table and held her chair for her before seating himself. When the soup and side-dishes had been served, she waved the servants away.

"So, what have you done in your life, Mr. De'Ath?" she said.

He seemed to be ready for her this time, for he answered entertainingly and fluently. He had, apparently, stayed in a gypsy encampment and danced at a wedding there. He had learned how to lay bricks and dig ditches. He had watched a prize fight and spent the night in the stable of an inn called the Duck and Spoon, because all the rooms were occupied by inebriated young gentlemen. He had sung questionable drinking songs with some farm labourers on market day and run away from the local watchmen. He had met a missionary clergyman on his way to Africa and had almost gone with him just for the adventure.

"Why didn't you?" Tabitha asked, fascinated.

The spellbinding light of fun faded from his eyes. "Oh, responsibilities, you know? And I don't think I would make a very good missionary. I would almost certainly be more interested in novel heathen beliefs than my own. But I am glad to count the clergyman amongst my new friends."

"Then this was recently?" she asked, surprised. She made a discovery. "It was *all* recently! You, sir, have slipped your leash."

He grinned, for all the world like a shy but mischievous schoolboy caught with his hand in the biscuit barrel. She knew a sudden urge to go with him as he followed his nose from place to place, seeing the world anew through his ever-curious perspective.

And then it came to her exactly what kind of leash he was escaping. The same one that had confined her for four years.

"Mr. De'Ath, are you married?"

She was annoyed with herself as soon as she had asked. She did not want to know if she was entertaining someone else's husband. He wore no rings of any kind.

But he shook his head, and his surprise seemed genuine. For some reason, she found it suddenly difficult to meet his warm, still-smiling gaze. Caught up in the humour of his tales, she had almost forgotten that she was dining alone with a uniquely attractive young man. But she was aware of him now. Far too aware.

Had he made her laugh to seduce her? It was a novel approach, but she found it difficult to attribute such calculation to him. The chief entertainment of his stories had been his own joy in each new character, each new situation.

A pity. I would not mind being seduced by such a man...

Yes, I would! I am known here, and I am a bare fifteen miles from Sark Park...

"Is something troubling you?"

His question took her by complete surprise. She pushed her half-eaten cherry pie away from her and let her eyelids droop.

"Good Lord, no," she drawled. "Very little ever troubles me."

But she must have let down her guard. Foolish, for she had always recognized the perception in his gaze—and kindness that was not, for some reason, unbearable.

"I shall not pry," he said with oddly charming diffidence, "but I would count it an honour to help you in any way I can."

"Quite the knight in shining armour," she said. "If only this damsel were distressed. Sadly, she is merely charmed."

"Is she?" he said wistfully.

Startled, she stared at him. Desire without demand, gentle and arousing...

Fortunately, the innkeeper's wife led the servants in just then to clear the table, leaving them only with the remains of their wine. While making idle conversation, Tabitha let an exciting idea wind around her mind and take root.

It was *not* impossible. She didn't think she had ever encountered kindness in a man before, certainly not in an attractive young man. In him, it was allied with discretion and those smiling, observant eyes... Those long, slender fingers now idly twisting the stem of his glass would be gentle on her skin, and so very pleasurable...

The door closed behind the inn servants, and she stopped talking. She had no idea what she had been saying anyway.

He set his glass down on the table and took her hand. Lightning fizzed through her veins.

He said, "I think you have been sad for a long time. I wish I could make you happy."

Oh God, what had he seen? And did it really matter?

For the first time, it didn't. Not with him.

"I am happier than I was," she managed.

"Now you are flattering me."

She searched his eyes and almost laughed. "You really don't know, do you?"

"Know what?"

"How devastating you are."

A crease twitched on his brow and vanished. His head dipped toward her, and she swayed nearer, her heart drumming.

But his head bowed lower to where their clasped hands rested on the table, and he kissed her fingers before releasing them. "I promised. No importuning, no seducing."

She sighed. "There he is again, that honourable, shining knight."

"I am not the man you think me."

"Why, what have you done?" she asked flippantly.

"Nothing." The inexplicable hint of bitterness in his voice confused her.

"Perhaps you should take the opportunities life offers before they are withdrawn."

He understood her. It was in the rueful quirk of his lips. "There is the grasping of opportunity, and there is taking advantage."

She laughed. "My dear sir, no one has *ever* taken advantage of me."

"I wish that were true. But then, I wish a lot of things. I am your friend, you know, and I hope you will be able to forgive me."

"I am more likely to forget you," she said.

She couldn't tell if it hurt him or not. It struck her that he was too good at hiding his feelings, no doubt through practice. He rose to his feet.

"May I escort you to your room?"

"I do not wish to go just yet."

"Then I thank you for your hospitality and bid you goodnight." He bowed to her.

She inclined her head in return, half-careless, half-mocking. It was her armour, carefully fashioned and almost impenetrable. But he could not know that, and she sensed his hurt, a hurt he did not deserve.

"Mr. De'Ath?"

He paused.

"I won't really forget you," she said.

There was a pause. "Nor I you," he replied. "Whatever happens."

She turned quickly to the door, but he had already gone.

"Whatever happens." What a curious thing to say.

JACK FELT EVERY STEP groan beneath his feet as he made his lonely way to bed. Since leaving Isley Place he had positively rejoiced in that alone-ness, no doctor's tonic to swallow, no valet fussing around him, no one looking in on him in the middle of the night to make sure he hadn't expired in his sleep.

For some reason, the beautiful woman in the parlour had wanted him. God knew he wanted her and with the kind of desire he had never known before, fierce and urgent yes, but with an added spice he could only call adoration. And he had the oddest feeling that making love to her would be the most exquisite adventure he would ever know.

Entering his room, he lit the lamp from the candle in his hand and went to stare sightlessly out of the window. Although their parting was trivial in the grand scheme of things, right now, it felt like loss, like tragedy. Not for the absence of one night in her bed, but for the impossibility of something he foolishly called love. And the happiness he would have striven to bring her. But if she ever found it, it could not be with him. For he knew who Tabitha was: the Dowager Countess of Sark, stepmother to Lady Lily, the girl he was bound to marry. And that would always keep them apart.

In fact, he could not even call on Lily just yet, because she was going to a party. He would wait another two or three weeks, he thought with relief. Which gave him time to recover before he had to meet Tabitha again as a stranger.

He picked up the newly-bought map from the table and spread it out on his bed. Where could he go next?

Chapter Three

Tabitha wasted too much time deciding just how to greet him in the morning, both to keep his friendship and to prove his rejection did not matter to her in the slightest. Eventually, she decided upon sleepy good humour and an exchange of cards at parting. Then she walked decisively downstairs for breakfast in her private parlour.

"Invite Mr. De'Ath to join me if he has risen," she told the innkeeper's wife.

"Oh, he's gone more than an hour, my lady," the woman said. "He asked to be remembered to you."

Her sense of desolation was ridiculous. She had known him a matter of hours. But they could have been friends as well as lovers. Without knowing it, that was what she had always been looking for.

"Oh, and there's a message from Sir Hubert, too—the magistrate. He'll be along before ten this morning."

"Excellent," Tabitha replied, as though the matter was at the forefront of her mind, which it wasn't. She had sent a message to him on her arrival in Cogglesworth, about the attempted hold-up, but since De'Ath had gone, she had little enough to tell the man.

As soon as she left Sir Hubert, she climbed into her waiting coach and set off on the last stage of her journey to Sark Park. The nearer she got, the deeper the sense of oppression that settled over her. It was an ugly feeling that she could never quite shake off, even though the old devil was dead. Neither his children nor his successor troubled her, yet somehow the ghost of her late husband never quite seemed to fade from the place.

The carriage drew up to the Dower House and Lily ran out to meet her.

"Tabbie! I'm so glad you're back!" she cried, throwing her arms around her stepmother. "I came down to wait for you, for so much has been happening and I wanted to tell you before Cousin Ralph gets his oar in. Come in, come in. I love that hat, Tab, did you buy it in Brighton?"

Lily half-dragged her into the house where she disentangled herself to greet her housekeeper and butler who had come here straight from the Brighton house while Tabitha travelled by easier stages.

Having ordered tea, Tabitha swept her stepdaughter into the drawing room and settled herself into her favourite chair, angled so that her back was to the big house where she had once lived with the earl her husband. Lily paced back and forth in front of her, twisting her hands together, as though, now that she finally had her stepmother's ear, she couldn't find the right words.

Tabitha waited patiently, for Lily was subject to crises and this one was unlikely to be insoluble. She wondered where Mr. De'Ath was, what he was doing, and if his horse had turned out to be the friend he hoped. A smile twitched at her lips for there had been something truly engaging about the man. Curiously, she no longer even felt embarrassed by his rejection, for she had read the struggle in his eyes, desire versus chivalry and chivalry had won. She was not worth such honour of course, but now that she thought of it, she rather liked that in him too. Her horseless knight...

"You have always said I should not marry until I wished," Tabitha said in a rush. "And that I might choose my own husband."

Tabitha blinked. "I insist upon it. Have you fallen madly in love?"

"Lord, no, quite the opposite." Lily threw herself into the chair nearest Tabitha's. "Cousin Ralph says I am betrothed."

Tabitha peered at Lily's tragic face more closely. "Did you agree?"

"No, of course I didn't."

"Then you are not."

"But apparently *Papa* agreed. He made the promise with the old duke before I was even born!"

"In writing?" Tabitha asked swiftly.

"I...I don't know. Does it matter?"

"A legal contract will be harder to repudiate, but we shall do it all the same."

Lily's face relaxed into smiles. "I said you would know just what to do."

"Which old duke are we talking about?" Tabitha cast her mind around for an unmarried one.

"Isbourne," Lily said with loathing.

Tabitha lifted one eyebrow. *Another De'Ath...* "He is too old even for Ralph, being dead these twenty years!"

"No, no, it's the son I'm supposed to marry. The late duke made the arrangement with Papa for one of his daughters. I am the only one left."

"Then why have we never heard this nonsense before?" Tabitha demanded.

"I don't know." Lily shifted discontentedly and scowled. "I was taken to meet him once, though. Ralph told me that and I asked Nurse about it. I remembered him then, a shocking milksop of a boy—he let me play with his toys but just read his book all the time I was there, even when Nurse took me outside to play. He didn't come." Her frown smoothed. "Still, I expect he wasn't allowed to, poor creature, or he might have expired at my feet which would probably have upset me. Although if he *had* expired, I would not now be in this predicament, would I?"

Tabitha's lip twitched involuntarily, but she kept the rest of her face grave.

"But only think, Tabbie! I *cannot* marry the Duke of Death, it would be torture. I am useless with invalids, and I would positively die myself of the tedium! He lives in this great, terrifying mausoleum of a place that makes our big house look like a cottage. Even Nurse said it must be haunted."

"Yes, well, the haunting or not is immaterial, since you are not going to marry the Duke of Death."

"Oh good." Lily sat back in her chair and grinned at her stepmother. "I knew you would save me. How do we get out of it?"

"I don't know yet. The first thing is to talk to Ralph."

"Well, I told them I was moving back over here with you, now that you were home, and we are both invited to dine at the big house."

Tabitha wrinkled her nose, for she went there as seldom as possible. On this occasion, it would have to be done. She changed the subject as though the last one was of little account.

"Well, we shall be off again in a couple of days, if you would still like to attend Lady Hawthorn's party with me?"

"Oh, of all things!" Lily declared, brightening immediately.

At eighteen, she was eager to go out into Society, to meet other young people, wear pretty clothes, dance, and enjoy herself. Ralph and his wife, on the excuse of mourning some distant relative, had postponed her debut this Season, refusing even Tabitha's offer to present Lily to the Queen and to the ton at her own expense. Of course, Tabitha could have taken her anyway, but she chose not to quarrel over it, instead reaching a compromise that they would introduce Lily gradually, via a few house parties this summer and autumn, with a view to a formal presentation next Season.

Tabitha wondered now if Ralph's reluctance had anything to do with this ducal betrothal that no one else seemed to know anything about. She began to roll up her metaphorical sleeves for the fight.

DRESSING WITH CARE, while Lily watched from the bed, fascinated, her chin resting on her clasped hands, Tabitha said, "You will be the perfect young lady, if you please, no defiance or arguments."

Lily shifted to display her demure white muslin gown.

"Yes, very suitable, but you're crushing it," Tabitha pointed out, and the girl hastily jumped up and shook out the gown, looking guilty.

"I suppose I have a good deal to learn," she said humbly.

"Don't learn too much," Tabitha said. "Natural manners are more appealing. You just have to find your own balance between propriety and *you*. But I know you will not disgrace yourself." It was not in the girl's nature or her upbringing. Lively and even mischievous she might be, but she was neither silly nor ill-natured.

Tabitha fastened her earrings and regarded herself in the mirror. Allison, her maid, who always stood back to allow her mistress to finish her own toilette, nodded and stepped forward to twitch a fold of her gown. She then adjusted Lily's gown and handed both ladies their reticules and shawls.

"Thank you, Allison," Tabitha said. "We shan't be late."

Since it was a fine night, they walked up to the house with no outerwear but their shawls draped from the elbows and were soon ushered into the dining room where it was the custom to gather at the opposite end to the great mahogany table. They did not sit in the uncomfortable chairs grouped there, but stood by the window until the countess chose to breeze in.

"Cousin Portia" as Tabitha had always known her, thoroughly enjoyed being countess and taking precedence at last over Tabitha. But today, she was at her most gracious, actually welcoming the dowager countess home and going so far as to kiss the air close to her cheek.

"How was your journey, my dear?" Portia asked, standing back as though examining Tabitha's health. She was a handsome woman inclined to stoutness and unfortunately addicted to frills and bold prints. Her slightly protuberant eyes were sharp, and her thin mouth pinched in repose.

"Not as eventful as it might have been. I was glad of my outriders to scare off a highwayman yesterday."

"Oh, my dear! What happened?" Portia demanded.

"You never told me that!" Lily exclaimed at the same time.

Cousin Ralph, Earl of Sark, chose to make his entrance at that point, very conscious of his own dignity and value—though financially speaking, Tabitha had begun to suspect that value was not high. Which may well have been the catalyst for reviving this bizarre betrothal, if it had ever existed.

"*Highwaymen?*" he exclaimed, pursing his lips as though the very word was an insult to his name.

"Oh, just the one," Tabitha said carelessly, "and the outriders only had to face him with their pistols for him to ride on—laughing, the impudent rogue. But then he had just had a spot of luck robbing some other poor devil, even taking his horse. I reported the incident to Sir Hubert at Cogglesworth, though I don't expect to hear any more of it. I merely mentioned it to Portia to make sure you don't decide to economize on outriders when you travel."

"Let us sit down," Portia said. "Dinner is about to be served."

Since every meal was served with tedious formality, the servants were present throughout and it was impossible to talk of anything more confidential than the weather, Brighton gossip, and the prospects of Lady Hawthorn's approaching party. During the last discussion, Tabitha was aware of the earl and countess exchanging glances and knew there would be difficulties extracting Lily. Difficulties, but no impediments, she promised herself.

At last, after the indifferent and rather meagre meal, the ladies left his lordship to his solitary port, and repaired to the drawing room where at last, as Tabitha's brother Barty might have put it, the gloves came off.

"I suppose Lily has already told you the news of her stunning betrothal?" Portia said, smiling with proud delight although her eyes remained hard.

"It certainly stunned me," Tabitha said mildly. "How on earth has this oddity come about?"

"Oh, it was all agreed before your time, Tabitha. And of course, his grace and our Lily are old friends."

Tabitha smiled. "I hardly think an hour's unsuccessful visit at the age of six constitutes a friendship. You and Ralph know my views on Lily's marriage. They have not changed."

"But he is a duke!"

"And when he dies there will be no dukedom."

"There will be children," Portia said. "Besides, I don't believe his grace is quite at death's door yet! According to Lord Hazlett, his grace's guardian, who has been corresponding with Sark, the duke is in considerably better health. In fact, he proposes to call on Lily at our convenience."

Tabitha closed her mouth on the retort she had been about to make. She glanced at Lily.

"I suppose," Portia said with heavy sarcasm, "you have no objection to his grace's calling?"

"None whatsoever. If Lily likes him and wishes to marry him, I shall, of course, reconsider my veto."

The light of battle in Portia's face faded into something of an anticlimax. She had expected more of a fight. However, tossing her head with a hint of triumph, she stretched her luck.

"So, you see, you must not take Lily to Lady Hawthorn's with you. It would be so insulting to his grace to find her gone when he came all that way to see her."

"On the contrary, Lily must keep her engagements. That is a basic requirement of good manners. The duke may wait here for her return or join us there. She cannot sit at home like some supplicant just in case he chooses to call."

Colour began to stain Portia's cheeks. "You misunderstand. His grace is not a sociable man. And only think how awkward it will be for them to meet with so many people observing their every word and action."

"It has always been quite normal for young people to meet in public," Tabitha said tartly. "If his grace does not wish it, he may postpone his visit for three weeks, or a month. When does he propose to come?"

Portia almost wriggled. "We are not quite sure. Lord Hazlett was a little vague, but he did say it would be very soon. Sark is convinced he will be here any day."

"Then be so good as to give me his lordship's direction—along with his grace's—and I shall write informing them of our convenience."

Portia's face was positively mottled. "That would be unforgivably rude when Sark has already written that we have no engagements and that his grace is welcome at any time!"

"Hardly. On the contrary, it will give you and Ralph time to entertain the man alone and form a true opinion of his suitability. We will, of course, take that into consideration."

"Oh, for goodness sake, Tabitha!" Portia burst out. "Anyone would think you did not want this honour, this brilliant match for our Lily!"

"I'm not sure that I do," Tabitha replied. "We can discuss it further when Lily has met him and got to know him a little. There is no rush, Portia, especially not since you tell me his grace has taken his foot out of the grave."

"There is no need to be vulgar."

"I beg your pardon for my inappropriate humour."

Portia met her gaze. "You are in her way, Tabitha," she said deliberately. "You can be removed, you know."

"You can try that," Tabitha said pleasantly, "but be aware the courts move very slowly —and expensively—especially with challenges. And I understand Ralph still has not received his Writ of Summons from the Lord Chancellor. Perhaps there is a challenge there, too."

She threw the barb out largely to annoy Portia, and from the countess's angry flush, she had struck closer to home than she had imagined.

Ralph had already adopted the title of earl and no one Tabitha knew had truly doubted the succession. But if there truly was a doubt, then that would also explain Ralph's rush to ally with a ducal family who would support his claim. Not that she could truly imagine such a scenario. Ralph just wanted all the acceptance he could grasp.

"Do you know," Tabitha drawled, "I am tired after my journey? I believe I must ask you to bid Ralph good night on our behalf. Thank you for your kind hospitality, Portia."

Lily jumped up with alacrity, and they were already out of the door before Portia could ring for them to be shown out.

Lily giggled. "As if we do not know the way! You were splendid, Tabbie."

"It's not the end of it," Tabitha warned. "We need to see whatever legal contract there is."

AS SHE HAD HOPED, RALPH produced a document the following morning, having trotted down from the big house apparently with that sole purpose. Tabitha glimpsed him from her morning room window.

Of course, he did not trot once he was indoors. He progressed into the room in a stately manner, ignoring her butler who had barely announced him. Tabitha rose civilly from her desk, where she had been writing letters, and invited him to sit.

Before he did so, he fished out a folded document from inside his coat and presented it to her.

"Portia tells me you are not in favour of this marriage for Lily, though I cannot imagine why you are so against such a brilliant match. Her dowry is not large for her rank, you know, and we never hoped for such a great marriage. But in point of fact, neither you nor I have a say in it. As you will see, it has already been decided."

She took the document from him with a murmur of thanks and sat down to read it.

"It is merely a copy," Ralph said grandly. "The original is with my solicitor."

The "contract" was a mere half page, and it was certainly not composed by anyone in the legal profession. In fact, Tabitha suspected it had been more in the nature of a drunken act of sworn friendship scrawled out by either Sark or Isbourne in a far less neat manner than the copy. She imagined the original peppered with ink blots and wine splashes, uneven lines of barely legible script. But if she could trust the copy, the original had been signed and dated by both parties on the same day in March 1787. And it did express the intention that the Duke of Isbourne's first born son and heir should marry a daughter of Lord Sark's.

"It is not witnessed," Tabitha observed. "And I very much doubt it can be enforced, particularly against the wishes of the participants, since neither of them are named and indeed had not even been born at the time."

"Nevertheless," Ralph said primly, "it is my duty to respect the wishes of my uncle and his friend, the late duke, which are quite clear from this document. And you will find you are wrong about the wishes of the participants."

"Am I? Young Isbourne is not exactly beating a path to your door, is he? He has not made an offer for Lily. At best, he plans to drop in to look her over at some point when he isn't too busy and his health is up to it."

Ralph flushed. "His grace is anxious to do his duty by the dukedom and the wishes of his father. Lord Hazlett assures me of that, and of the fond memories of Lily which the duke retains."

"Lily doesn't. She remembers him as a sick and dull milksop, and you know she has a horror of the sick room since her mother died. It won't work, Ralph."

Ralph's eyes narrowed. "I won't have you standing in her way, Tabitha."

The threat was not subtle. There was indeed a Lisle bully beneath the excessive dignity. But he would never bully Tabitha.

"As I told Portia, I will receive him if and when he comes. If he offers for her, and if Lily likes him well enough for marriage, and if you and I find him unexceptionable, then I will never stand in her way."

"But you are removing her just when he is most likely to visit! Leave her behind and go alone to your wretched party. You usually do."

This was hardly true, and his flushed face told her he knew it. But she found it more interesting that he did not suggest that Tabitha should stay too. He did not want her here when the young couple met. In fact, he probably hoped to have them safely married by special license before Tabitha returned from Hawthorn Court.

"I have promised her she may come. I am not dragging her away from a beloved suitor, Ralph. She wants company of her own age and a little gaiety."

"You are not a fit person to be in charge of an innocent young girl," he said furiously.

Tabitha smiled. "But we are all compelled, are we not, by our duty to honour the wishes of my late husband, your dear uncle? And *that* document *is* binding."

THE FOLLOWING DAY, as the sun peeped over the horizon, Tabitha and Lily set out for Hawthorn Court. Behind them, in the old coach, came Allison, Tabitha's maid, with a mountain of baggage. As they drove briskly toward the main drive, the big house seemed to stare at them malevolently. Tabitha thought a curtain twitched at the upper window where the earl's rooms were located. She shivered, for she sensed dislike on his part had just turned into enmity.

It was nothing to do with wanting the best for Lily, or even dislike of Tabitha's defiance. He only cared for money and his own dignity, so for some reason he must really need this marriage. Lily's wealthy suitor must have promised Ralph some outrageously generous settlements, settlements that would benefit him personally.

She looked forward to finally meeting this so-called Duke of Death and discovering exactly why.

Chapter Four

The trouble began largely because Lily was so excited to see the sea that Tabitha instructed the coachman to follow the coast roads as far as possible.

After all, this whole expedition was for Lily's benefit. Tabitha, beyond the pleasure of reunion with Louisa Hawthorn and one or two other old friends, was infinitely bored with the same-ness of country house parties. And in this case, she would have to be on her best behaviour to chaperone Lily properly. Perhaps it would be more amusing seeing everything through Lily's innocent eyes.

Like seeing the world through Mr. De'Ath's almost child-like eagerness, with his enjoyment of bricklayers' jokes and Romany weddings, and even robbery on the king's highway. But there was no point in thinking of him.

Unfortunately, changing the direct route known to the coachman meant that by evening, when they were all hungry, they were lost. Struggling inland again in the presumed direction of Hawthorn Court, they found the roads in a shocking state and almost impassible, alternately water-logged into mud, or so dry and rutted that even the excellently-sprung travelling coach bounced painfully over them.

Worse, there were no signposts. The odd local encountered on the road merely gaped and shrugged when James the coachman inquired for the Firkin Inn, where Tabitha had reserved rooms and meals. In this way, she had planned to arrive at Hawthorn Court at a civilized time the following day.

Even before darkness fell into damp blackness beneath the lowering clouds, Tabitha was convinced they were going in circles.

She stuck her head out of the window. "Do you see *anything*, James?"

"There's a few lights 'way to the left there," James said grimly. "But they seem to be moving."

He was right. She could make out a ragged little row of them, pale and indistinct as if very far away in the direction she imagined to be the sea.

"Head towards them," Tabitha ordered. "They must be going somewhere!"

"I'll try," James said grimly.

For the next half hour, the carriage bumped and slogged over even worse tracks, some of which were barely wide enough, as James tried to intercept the lights. The tracks did not always co-operate, running too straight or bending in the wrong direction and neither did the lights which frequently vanished from view altogether.

"Perhaps they are lights on fishing boats," Lily said, "and we are just driving back to the coast."

It had crossed Tabitha's mind as well, especially since the clouded skies deprived James of his normally excellent sense of direction.

"I told Ralph and Portia you needed amusement," she said.

Lily laughed. "I think I need supper more."

"Think of the poor horses... Oh, look, a signpost!"

The coach's lanterns had indeed lit up a sign for a place called Garth, pointing along a wider track to the right. The horses came to a halt, and again Tabitha stuck her head out of the window.

"Promising!" she called hopefully to James.

"Maybe. But the lights are to the left and much closer than they were. Which way do you want me to go? No guarantees there'll be an inn at this Garth place which I've never heard of. It might even just be a farm. On the other hand, at least it's somewhere definite."

Lily was peering out of the other window. "It says it's only one mile to Garth."

Tabitha, watching the lights with growing curiosity, rubbed one finger across her lips. She dropped her hand into her lap. "Then let's turn left and follow the lights. If they lead nowhere, we at least know where Garth is."

James shrugged and urged the horses forward and to the left.

"What a very odd decision," Lily said. "You just want to know what the lights are."

"Well, they have come quite a long way, and I don't believe whoever is carrying them has been using any roads. But I won't drag us far. If they lead nowhere, we'll return to Garth." Of course, whether or not they could turn the carriage was another matter. Perhaps she had let curiosity lead her into the poorest of decisions. Again.

However, they had not gone very far at all along the left-hand track when yet another light glimmered through the trees. The track bent toward it and beneath the light which hung over a stone arch, an extremely dirty sign proclaimed—or at least murmured indistinctly—The Headless Horseman Inn.

"Tabitha, you are a genius," Lily said in delight. "How on earth did you know?"

"Of course I didn't. I was following my nose."

James guided the tired horses under the stone arch into a somewhat unwelcoming yard. No one ran to greet them. The house was a decent size, though apart from one downstairs light, it appeared to be in darkness. One side of the yard seemed to be a stable block, judging by the equine snorts and stamps within. The opposite side consisted of indistinct outbuildings.

"House!" James roared and climbed down from his box.

The door of the main house opened abruptly. A skinny lad peered out. "Billy?"

"No," James growled, opening the coach door and letting down the steps. "But we'll be requiring accommodation for two ladies, myself, and four horses. Jump to it, boy—the horses are dead on their hooves!"

Abruptly, the skinny boy was shoved aside and a huge barrel of a man with long, curling side whiskers strode out with a lantern. His gaze swept over the new arrivals and, as James deliberately closed the carriage door, the muddied Sark crest.

He did not look pleased. In fact, for a moment, his scowl denoted extreme irritation, but he bowed all the same. "Welcome to the Headless Horseman. I'm Rains, your host. Come in, come in, and my wife will look after you, ladies. Shift yourself, Harry, and let's see to these horses..."

The innkeeper's sudden hurry was a relief to Tabitha, who was more than happy to step into the house. There, a plump woman was busy lighting candles in wall sconces around a big, open room which smelled of tallow, tobacco, and stale beer.

"So sorry, ma'am, we wasn't expecting guests of quality," the woman babbled. "I'll take you up directly and Harry will bring your bags. I hope you don't mind sharing a bedchamber, only with no notice..."

"That will be acceptable," Tabitha said, looking about her. "Though we would appreciate a private parlour."

"Alas, ma'am, I cannot help you there! But it is a lovely big bedchamber, and I'll be more than happy to serve you there myself. A nice bit of mutton stew before you retire?"

"Thank you," Tabitha said graciously, although the meal did not sound terribly appetizing.

The woman, presumably Mrs. Rains, began to lead them toward the stairs, just as Harry brought in the bags.

"Is that all you've got?" she demanded, stopping in her tracks.

Tabitha raised her eyebrows. "It is adequate for tonight. We shan't be staying longer."

"The rest of our baggage went ahead to Hawthorn Court," Lily added, as though made suddenly nervous by the woman's disapproval, though it did not appear to stem from an excess of respectability. Tabitha suspected the woman had been hoping for large gratuities or even, more worryingly, thieving opportunities.

"We got lost going too far along the coast," Lily explained. "We were so pleased to come upon your house."

Mrs. Rains sniffed, swiped up the bags from the floor, since Harry had rushed outside again, and led the way up the dusty staircase.

"Do you have many guests?" Tabitha asked, as they passed several closed doors along a dark passage and around the corner to another, past a half-glass door that seemed to give onto an outside staircase.

Mrs. Rains did not light any of the sconces as she went, relying on her own single candle which cast eerie, flickering shadows up the bare stone walls. Tabitha and Lily stayed close to each other and to their guide's light.

"It varies," Mrs. Rains replied vaguely. "And of course we're refurbishing the old place..."

"Not so as you'd notice," Lily murmured in Tabitha's ear, eyeing the cobwebs.

Mrs. Rains threw open the door at the very end of the third passage and beamed with triumph. "There, you see, our most superior bedchamber!" She dropped their bags on the floor at her feet while they followed her inside.

As she moved across the room, lighting the lamp on the table and two wax candles on the walls, they saw that the room was indeed large, containing two huge and ancient four-poster beds, a marble-topped chest of drawers with a washing bowl, and, built into the wall, a large cupboard for hanging clothes which Mrs. Rains showed them with some pride. There was also a table and two upright chairs.

Compared with the rest of the house, the chamber was surprisingly sweet-smelling and airy, which was due no doubt to the wide-open window which Mrs. Rains shut with a slam before closing the curtains.

"Best keep the cold and the rain out. Will you have the fire lit? It might smoke a bit."

"No, I believe we will be warm enough," Tabitha said hastily. "This will do very well."

"Then I'll go and see about your supper, Mrs...?" She waited hopefully.

"Lady Sark," Lily supplied. "And I am Lady Lily Lisle."

"Oh my," said Mrs. Rains with genuine awe. "We don't normally have guests of such quality. We're too out of the way, see? Well, you make yourselves comfortable, my ladies..." She waddled off, closing the door carefully behind her.

"What a strange inn," Lily remarked. "It looks as if it's on its last legs." She sank down on the bed. "As am I."

A small, slightly grubby girl brought a jug of warm washing water, which she left on top of the chest before effacing herself. Both women almost pounced on the water and were still drying their hands when Mrs. Rains appeared with a laden tray.

Their meal smelled surprisingly good, and it came with a jug of rather excellent wine.

"They're certainly used to catering to someone's expensive tastes," Tabitha remarked, setting down her glass. She began to suspect the origins of those lights they had followed.

While Lily consumed the cold apple pie and cream that followed the stew, Tabitha went to the window and slipped behind the heavy curtains to peer outside. However, the view was from the back of the house, looking away from the sea. To her far left, a faint glow seemed to imply that James had been given a berth at the back too, but above the stable block. She knew he would not have retired if his horses had not been well enough cared for, so she did not need to worry about them either.

On the other hand, she saw no familiar pattern of bobbing lights, so whoever they belonged to, they had not passed the Headless Horseman. She wondered if they were still advancing. On sudden impulse, she turned and took one of the spare candles she always carried when she travelled and lit it from one of the wall sconces.

"I'm just going to explore and walk off this dinner," she said casually. "Will you stay awake long enough to finish the pie?"

"Maybe not," Lily said with a sleepy smile. Her unease about the inn seemed to have been overcome by food or exhaustion or both. "Just be careful, Tabbie—it seems an odd sort of a place to me."

And to Tabitha. Wrapping herself in a shawl against the drafts, she took a candle and left the room. She walked along the passage to where she had seen the half-glass door and the outside staircase. Although the door was locked, the key had been left inserted, so she turned it carefully to avoid any loud clicks, then slipped outside onto the stone landing.

The stairs were at the side of the house, and she peered out into the darkness toward the front. Her heart thudded once with excitement, for there were the moving lights, very close now.

She flitted silently down the stairs, abandoned her candle on the bottom step, and moved through the darkness at the base of the building toward the main yard. She had just crept as far as the corner when her skin prickled.

Someone was just around that corner. She could sense their breath, their heat. Considering her suspicions of the house and the approaching lights, she really did not want to fall over any lookouts and betray that she was spying. She eased carefully back, listening to the slow, gentle thud of hooves on soft ground.

Inevitably, curiosity got the better of her. Sensing that the other presence had moved away, she crept forward again, craning her neck, and watched as an array of men with lanterns and ponies ambled through the arch and into the yard. Tabitha almost crowed with triumph, for the ponies were all burdened with casks and baskets of bottles. The lights they had been following belonged to smugglers, moving from their landing beach to this inn where, presumably, the contraband was stored before being distributed. She could not imagine the Headless Horseman got enough trade to justify so much brandy and wine and whatever else the poor ponies carried. A few darkly-dressed men led the ponies. Another more dignified fellow walked in their midst beside a gangly boy.

Something moved too close to her, treading on her toe, and abruptly she was thrust back against the wall, both hands gripped captive above her head and a gloved hand hard across her mouth.

Terrified, she was held too strongly to struggle, though she kicked instinctively at her attacker's shins. She heard his breath hiss, but he only moved closer, restricting the rest of her body with his own. She stared up into her attacker's face, waiting with angry helplessness for the blow of fist or knife.

Her brows flew up. The rest of her suddenly sagged. For enough light now spilled around from the yard for her to recognize the features of Jack De'Ath.

The gentle eyes that had disturbed her dreams were unexpectedly hard. And then they changed to warm astonishment. At the same time, his teeth gleamed, and his hand fell away from her face. He bent his head and covered her mouth with his.

LILY, HAVING GUILTILY consumed both portions of apple pie, felt slightly sick and stood up to walk it off. She looked forward to bed, but the inn made her so uneasy that she didn't want to retire before Tabitha returned and locked their chamber door. What took her so long? Was there really so much of the inn to explore?

Well, it did seem to be an odd place, big and rambling with no guests, extremely plain food, and wine worthy of her father's table. No doubt the last was smuggled, a crime that most people she knew seemed to regard with indulgence—decent bottles being of greater importance than either the King's revenue or the ongoing war with France.

Eventually, after a few circuits of the room, she decided to go in search of Tabitha and find out what was so wretchedly interesting that it had to keep them from their soft feather beds. Copying her step-mother, she threw a shawl about her shoulders, lit one of the spare candles, and opened the bedchamber door.

She gasped and almost shut it again, for outside the door on the right, only a few yards down the passage, stood a man looking directly at her.

For a moment, they both seemed to be paralyzed. The candle he grasped lent his face an oddly sinister tone, until he said, "I beg your pardon, ma'am. I did not mean to startle you."

She smiled with relief, for his speech alone proved he was a gentle-man. And now that she could think again, she realized he was young and in military uniform, with a shock of fair hair and a most pleasing countenance—not quite handsome perhaps, but very agreeable.

He bowed. "Allow me to introduce myself? Lieutenant Nathaniel Meade, at your service."

She curtseyed. "Lily Lisle."

"What a pretty name."

"Do you think so? My cousin says it makes me sound like a flower girl in Covent Garden."

He laughed. "Hardly! Are you looking for Mrs. Rains? May I escort you?"

"Actually, I was looking for my stepmother, who went to explore quite fifteen minutes ago..."

To her surprise, he seemed to understand her unease. "Yes, it's a rum sort of place, is it not? I was just going to step downstairs and have some supper. Perhaps your stepmother is there. I don't believe there are any other public rooms."

With some relief—for he seemed to be a very comfortable, unthreatening sort of young man—she closed the bedchamber door and walked with him. Which was when she realized he was limping.

"Are you injured, sir?" she asked in quick sympathy.

"Oh, not anymore," he said cheerfully. "They've been happily digging shrapnel out of my leg for weeks, but apparently it is all removed now. I wanted to go back to the Peninsula, but the doctors have insisted on two weeks more rest."

"Here?" she asked, appalled.

He grinned. "Lord, no, but since the doctors didn't define what sort of rest they meant, I've been trying out driving my brother's curricle about. I got lost taking the back roads to Hawthorn Court."

"Why, so did we!"

Delighted by this coincidence, it took her some time to notice that there were more voices in the common room downstairs. As one, they paused, leaning over the balustrade to see those gathered below: a well-dressed man in an exquisitely cut coat, a boy of around fourteen, similarly dressed, and another man who appeared to be a servant. They were all talking urgently in French when Mrs. Rains came barrelling in from the kitchen bearing a tray which she slammed down on the nearest table in order to glare up at Lily and Lieutenant Meade.

"What the devil are you doing there?" she demanded angrily.

JACK HAD FOLLOWED THE lights from the beach, at first from mere curiosity about the nature of "free trading," and then with the suspicion that more than mere brandy was being smuggled here. With his suspicions confirmed by snatches of French on the breeze, and the fact that three of the party he had followed did no actual work, he slipped back around the corner of the inn to decide what to do about it.

Encountering another body there, literally underfoot, scared the life out of him, and he reacted from pure instinct. Having never indulged in any physical violence more dangerous than punching his pillow, he had no plan and no real intention to hurt. His main concern was silence, though even as he acted, it struck him that if this was one of the smugglers or their allies at the inn, then he was already caught. His physical strength was largely untried and unknown.

And the fellow wriggled like a desperate eel.

As Jack tightened his grip, imprisoning the sneak's body with his own, grasping the small hands against the wall, clamping his hand across the mouth, which seemed very low down, he realized two things very quickly. This was not a fellow at all—she had far too many curves and skirts, and her perfume was inexplicably familiar. He leaned his head to the side to let the light from the front of the house touch her face above his hand, and relief and pleasure reacted without permission.

Tabitha. He didn't know if the word was on his lips or merely inside his head. It was just so unexpected and so wonderful that it seemed the most natural thing in the world to kiss her.

Only it wasn't, of course; it was entirely *wrong,* and the kiss was as fleeting as it was stunning. The flutter of her parted lips was indescribably sweet but barely more than an impression as he freed her at once. Her hands fell to her sides, and he ached for the loss of her soft, luscious curves against him...

She blinked and pushed around him to see what was going on in the yard.

Abruptly, reality rushed back on him, and he peered over her head. The pack ponies were being led toward the outbuildings, leaving only the two men he had overheard speaking French, and the boy who accompanied them. The innkeeper's wife was all but dragging them inside.

Jack moved back several yards, drawing Tabitha with him.

"What on earth are you doing here?" he demanded.

"Staying at the inn, of course. You?"

"I followed the lights from the coast."

Her lips twitched and she remembered to drawl this time. "So did we. No wonder the wine is good. The brandy will be excellent too."

"It could well be more than that," he said. "I don't suppose you know the way to the nearest town?"

"Don't inform on the Gentlemen. It will make you unpopular, and it will upset supplies for the rest of us."

"You don't understand. They're not just smuggling brandy. They're smuggling French people."

It was too dark now to see her face, but he heard her intake of breath. "With what purpose?"

"Who knows? Spying at a guess. Sabotage."

"Oh dear... That *would* be a much bigger problem. But how do you know they are French?"

"I heard them speaking while I followed them."

"Lots of people speak French," she said, "especially when they don't want the lower orders to understand. I've been known to do it myself."

It was something he hadn't thought of, so he spared the theory a moment's consideration. "It did not sound like Englishmen speaking French," he said cautiously. He could tell the difference, having had both English and French tutors in that language. "And they certainly came off the small boats along with brandy. But perhaps I've jumped to conclusions."

"And perhaps not," she said urgently. "This is a very odd inn, Jack. It's large and spacious and yet most of it smells unused, and we appear to be the only guests. We weren't exactly welcomed with open arms. There are lots of rooms, yet Lily and I were shoved into the same one at the very back of the house and strongly encouraged to dine there—kept out of the way, in other words."

His name on her lips gave him a pleasurable little frisson, though he tried to concentrate on her words. "There are some inns that are little more than dens of thieves," he said.

"Were you robbed in one of them, too?"

"No, I was warned off just in time by a more experienced traveller who sold rather charming under-garments for ladies. I don't like your being here."

Her eyes were alight with laughter, though whether at his caution or his under-clothes salesman, he could not tell. He just felt the effect in the pit of his stomach. And lower. He tried to think.

"I shall stay here, too," he said decisively. "It will take me only five minutes to fetch my horse." He began to move toward the courtyard wall by the stables, over which he had climbed in the first place.

"Wait," she hissed after him. "What if they don't let you in?"

"I shall be too important to keep out."

Chapter Five

As she watched him clamber up the corner of the stable and the yard wall, using footholds from both, his dark figure looked more ungainly than she had ever seen him, as though he had never climbed as a boy. Which was odd for someone of such an adventurous spirit. Still, he got there, for she heard the faint thud on the other side of the wall. She just hoped he hadn't broken his ankle.

She realized with surprise that it had begun to rain, more of a lazy drizzle than a downpour. She pulled the shawl over her head and hastened back to the outside steps. As she retrieved her candle, still mercifully alight, and ran up, she hoped no one had locked the door. Hopefully, they had all been too busy with their delivery of brandy and French speaking gentlemen.

The door opened easily, and she locked it carefully behind her before creeping back toward her bedchamber. She could hear no voices below or anywhere else in the dark house.

She shivered. She did not like the Rains couple at all. There was a hardness, a ruthlessness about their eyes. She could imagine them regarding two aristocratic women as too silly and too important to do away with. But what of Jack? A solitary traveller with no obvious connections and somewhat physically fragile...although there had been strength in the arms that had pinned her to the wall.

Her stomach plunged all over again as she remembered the all too brief caress of his mouth...

She hurried on around the corner, shining her candle into all the shadows it would reach. It was with considerable relief she finally slipped back inside their own room and quietly closed the door.

"Lily? We need to make some excuse to..." She trailed off, looking rather wildly around the room in search of her stepdaughter. "Lily, where the *devil*..."

She even opened the hanging cupboard and looked under the beds, just in case the girl had taken fright at something, but her blood was running cold. Throwing off the damp shawl, she took up her candle again and marched back down the passage.

Emerging into unexpected light on the landing, she blinked at the scene lit up below her.

Three weary, travel-stained gentlemen stood in a huddle to her right, gawping with varying degrees of alarm at Mrs. Rains who stood, hands on hips, in the middle of the room, glaring up the steps, not at Tabitha, but at Lily—*thank you, God!*—who seemed to have halted near the foot of the stairs beside a complete stranger in army uniform.

"Is there no food to be had at your hostelry, madam?" the officer was asking with a fair degree of irritation.

"'Course there is," Mrs. Rains answered aggressively, "but *she's* already had hers, and you was asleep!"

"I am now awake and hungry, and if the lady requires a glass of milk, I really do not see why she should not have one."

Mrs. Rains, becoming aware of Tabitha's candle and her movement toward the stairs, seemed to swear beneath her breath.

Lily and the officer both glanced around too. Before her stepdaughter could blurt something like, *There you are,* Tabitha hurried into speech.

"Why is this taking so long, Lily? If there is no milk in the house..."

"Lord lumme, of course there's milk," Mrs. Rains broke in. "I just got to serve these poor gents first, who've been travelling all day. Sit down, gentlemen, Rains will be in directly. The table is set for you just where you are..."

She moved to heft up a laden tray from the table nearer the kitchen door—or what Tabitha supposed was the kitchen door. "I'll bring it up," she snapped at the three on the stairs.

"That won't be necessary," Tabitha said regally, sailing the rest of the way downstairs and sweeping Lily and her unknown swain with her.

He was a pleasant-faced young man, who managed somehow to look pale beneath bronzed skin. It might have been a trick of the candlelight, but Tabitha suspected he had been injured, a suspicion confirmed when he limped aside and bowed to her.

"Oh, Tabbie," Lily said brightly, "this is Lieutenant Meade who is also staying here. I met him in the passage. Sir, my stepmother, Lady Sark."

"I am pleased to meet you, Lieutenant," Tabitha said, glancing at the other men in the room.

She found the adults still standing, watching her as if stunned, although the accompanying boy had thrown himself eagerly onto the nearest chair at the table. When his elders bowed to the ladies, he sprang up again and bowed too, gracefully enough to have been taught. Although tall, he seemed to be younger than she had first supposed, surely no older than thirteen or so.

Interesting. Did spies and saboteurs normally bring their children along?

Rather to her surprise, the oldest of the three men walked toward her and bowed again. "Lady Sark? Allow me to introduce myself. My name is Smith."

Oh, unimaginative! Although he spoke in perfect English, without the accents betrayed by most of the emigrees she had met.

"How do you do, Mr. Smith?" She looked pointedly at the boy.

"My son, Edward."

Certainly another English name, though he may not have been born with it. The boy bowed again, his eyes wide now, as if he had started to pay attention. The third man had stepped back and was not introduced—presumably a servant.

"My stepdaughter, Lady Lily Lisle," Tabitha said languidly.

"Dinner is served," Mrs. Rains growled as she crashed the last dish down on the table.

"We shall wait here," Tabitha informed her, taking a seat at an empty table not too close to the Frenchmen, "for our milk."

"A small plate of cold cuts, or leftovers, with small beer, is all I require," Lieutenant Meade added.

"Do join us, Lieutenant," Tabitha invited, just as the door burst open in a gust of damp wind, and Jack De'Ath strode in, slamming the door behind him. He took off his hat and shook himself like a dog.

"Who the b-devil are you?" Mrs. Rains demanded.

Jack regarded her with unexpected hauteur. "The name is Johns, but you won't know it since I have not reserved rooms. I have merely got separated from my people and need somewhere to stay for the night."

"We're full up," Mrs. Rains said shortly. "It's less than two miles to the tavern in Garth. They'll take you in."

As if she had not spoken, Jack said, "I shall have a bite of supper, and be sure the sheets are aired. Do send someone to see to my horse. There's no one in the stables."

Mrs. Rains scowled direly, her mouth opening and closing several times. Jack raised his eyebrow as though surprised to see her still in the room. She threw up her hands and stormed off to the kitchen, muttering.

Jack who, much to Tabitha's amusement, carried the important gentleman role with surprising splendour, looked about him in a leisurely fashion. He nodded distantly to the Frenchmen, and to those now seated at Tabitha's table.

Tabitha's lips twitched uncontrollably.

Mr. De'Ath—now apparently Mr. Johns—gave no sign of recognition, but hung his hat on the stand by the door and languidly unbuttoned his overcoat.

Mrs. Rains re-entered the room with surprising speed, and this time the huge barrel-shaped figure of her husband followed. Both bore trays and looked thunderous. The woman slapped two mugs of milk in front of Tabitha and Lily, and one of watery beer before Lieutenant Meade, then stepped aside to let her husband deliver a plate of familiar mutton stew to the officer.

Rains was breathing quickly, and his greasy hair was damp. But though his eyes were like flint he turned politely enough to the newest arrival. "Where would you care to sit, sir?"

"You are welcome to join us, sir," Tabitha said amiably.

Jack inclined his head. "You are kind." He sat in the vacant chair beside her. "My name is Johns."

"So I heard. Mine is Sark. This is my stepdaughter, Lady Lily, and Lieutenant Meade."

At least she had the pleasure of surprising him. His widening eyes flew to Lily and fixed upon her face. And that was when she felt her first ever pangs of monstrous, unbearable jealousy.

JACK HAD RATHER ENJOYED playing the haughty nobleman that his uncles and tutors had always wanted him to be. If he felt any resentment to see the dashing young officer sitting on Tabitha's other side, well, he had always known his limitations. Who the devil was the man to her?

But it was the presence of Lily that made him gawp so stupidly when he should have been prepared for it. Tabitha had told him when they first met that she was going home to collect her stepdaughter, but the fact had got lost somehow in the affair of the smugglers and the ridiculous, blazing happiness of being with her again so unexpectedly.

Lady Lily was still a remarkably pretty girl, though he doubted he would ever have recognized her from the six-year-old in pigtails and short skirts. There appeared to be some lively humour in her eyes and good nature in the curve of her lips.

Pulling himself together, he inclined his head to her and to Lieutenant Meade and let the innkeeper set a plate of stew in front of him.

"Wine, if you please," he said in the tones of one who is always obeyed. "And don't forget my poor horse."

The innkeeper's smile was so fixed that it looked more like a snarl, though he said, "Of course not, sir, we're seeing to him now."

The *we* troubled him. He hoped it was not the smugglers helping out for they were rough fellows, and he had grown fond of this horse. He resolved to go and check on him as soon as the meal was finished.

He barely noticed what he ate, although his entire household would have been scandalized by its plebian nature. He was too overwhelmed by his internal rejoicings to have Tabitha beside him, by the discomfort of Lily's presence, and by the mystery of the smuggled Frenchmen at the next table.

He observed the three of them from the corner of his eye while the conversation went on around his own table. He had the impression that the silent Frenchmen were listening too, though what they could learn from the tale of Lieutenant Meade's injury on the Peninsula several weeks ago, or the expected company at Lady Hawthorn's party, was debateable.

He was, however, glad to hear that Meade was not the ladies' escort, but someone merely encountered at the inn, who had got lost while making his own way to Hawthorn Court. He also noted that the young officer's eyes tended to stray more often to Lily than to Tabitha during lulls in the conversation. Perhaps another man making sheep's eyes at the ducal betrothed should not have pleased him. It could certainly make things more messy in the future.

For now, he decided to concentrate on the more urgent matter of the smuggled Frenchmen who, when they did speak to each other, did so in such low voices that he could not even make out which language they were speaking, let alone what they said. He was mulling over a few conversational gambits to draw them in when the oldest of the Frenchmen rose from his table and walked purposefully toward them.

He bowed. "Lady Sark."

"Mr. Smith," Tabitha returned graciously.

Smith? Seriously?

"Forgive my intrusion, but you may have gathered your name was familiar to me. I used to know a Lord Sark, many years ago. Althorpe was his Christian name."

"My late husband."

"Ah, I am very sorry to hear that. My condolences."

"You are too kind." Tabitha met the Frenchman's gaze limpidly. "I am surprised you did not know. It was more than two years ago."

"Alas, I have been abroad for many years. And the war has made British newspapers so difficult to acquire in Canada."

"Canada," Tabitha repeated.

"Indeed yes. I have lived there for more than twenty years. My son was born there."

Jack decided to move things along. "How very interesting," he murmured. "I had no idea that they made brandy in Canada."

Mr. Smith cast him a quick glance, rather engagingly rueful. "Hush, my friend, I am told the revenue men are everywhere. They do not make brandy in Canada, of course—or, at least, nothing you or I might recognize as such—and it would certainly make an unnecessarily long smuggling route from France to England. But consider the difficulties of His Majesty's loyal subjects shipwrecked off Brittany. There were limited routes home, and we were lucky enough to find one. So who is the earl now? Althorpe's son?"

Tabitha sipped her wine. "Althorpe was granted only daughters, of whom Lily here is the youngest. It is his nephew who inherited. Bramley's son."

"Ah, I see... Well, it has been very pleasant to speak to the wife of such an old friend. I do hope we meet again."

"As do I," Tabitha said cordially. "Perhaps we might hear more of your adventures."

"I trust so." Smith bowed to her and to the company in general and walked away to be met by Rains, lumbering through from the kitchen once more to show Smith's party the way.

Jack ate another forkful of the stew.

"And they've gone the other way along the passage," Tabitha murmured beside him, "to rooms at the front of the house. I suppose that is another reason why we are at the back."

"You were never meant to see them," Jack agreed, "let alone speak to them."

"Or everything could just be about the brandy and an unfortunate shipwreck."

"You believe Smith's story?" Jack asked.

"I'm not sure I believe anything he says, though to be sure he does not sound remotely French."

"Until you hear him speak in that language. He must have lived there many years." He broke off, becoming belatedly aware that Lily and the lieutenant were watching them in astonishment, their eyes shifting from one to the other to follow the quick conversation. He gave a diffident smile, forgetting his new role.

"Tabbie, do you and Mr. Johns know each other?" Lily demanded. "I mean, before this evening?"

"We met once upon a previous journey," Tabitha said airily. She lowered her voice again. "And we discovered earlier this evening that we shared the same suspicions about this house."

"So *that* is where you went," Lily said.

"And the same suspicions about his lordship's old friend there?" Meade asked.

"I can't imagine Papa making a friend of a mere Mr. Smith who went to Canada," Lily said frankly. "I think he made that up as an excuse to talk to you."

"Yes, but why?" Tabitha wondered.

Lily laughed. "Oh, Tabbie, why do you think?"

"You mean he is pursuing my widow's portion?"

"Not quite. I can see I am going to have to take you in hand at Lady Hawthorn's. Do *you* go to Hawthorn Court, Mr. Johns?"

Jack blinked. "Oh, no. I am not acquainted with Lady Hawthorn."

"I'm sure we could arrange that," Tabitha drawled. "You seem to be just the sort of gentleman she would like to be acquainted with."

Jack met the mocking gaze. "Why do I have the feeling that is not a compliment?"

Meade grinned. "I'm sure it is, you know. According to my mother and sisters, hostesses are always looking for eligible, unattached young gentlemen."

"Sadly, I qualify on none of those grounds," Jack said, "except youth, and time will take care of that. I am, in fact, expected elsewhere."

Which was true enough, although it pierced his heart to see the gleam in Tabitha's eyes fade. It was only for an instant, for she smiled as she pushed her untouched wine aside.

"Come, my love," she said to Lily. "We must say goodnight."

It was time, past time, that he told her the truth. And yet before Meade, he felt tongue tied. Instead, rising when she and Lily did, he murmured, "I have to follow Smith."

"Of course you do. Do keep us informed." She barely looked at him, merely bestowed a smile upon Meade. "We look forward to seeing you tomorrow, Lieutenant. Good night."

She was walking away from him, and it was only right. He had made promises that he would offer for Lily, if she did not dislike him. The girl might even expect it. At any rate, it appeared to be his duty. Lying to her, of course, was hardly a great start to their relationship. In fact, his irresponsible adventure was threatening misery all round.

Or perhaps Tabitha had merely dismissed him from her thoughts. After all, she was a lady of sophistication and must have men in constant pursuit.

"Sir, are you well?" Meade broke into his thoughts.

Immediately, Jack smoothed his brow and produced a smile. "Oh, perfectly. Forgive me, I was wool gathering."

Meade leaned forward. "About our friends?" He nodded toward the next table.

"Yes."

"What exactly is the problem? Because he came via France?"

"In war time, smuggling has become more than a revenue problem," Jack said. "If goods can come in and out unchecked, so can people."

Meade stared at him with some respect. "Good God. I never thought of that."

"I have read certain reports," Jack said apologetically. Although he had never formally taken his seat in the House of Lords, the influence of his title and his guardians ensured he was kept dutifully informed.

"But the man sounds as English as you or I."

"I have heard him speak French too, like a native. Hardly a crime, I grant you, but it does raise certain suspicions concerning his story."

"He must surely report his arrival to the authorities... What do you intend to do?"

Jack almost fell off his chair in surprise. Had anyone *ever* asked him his intentions before? He was much more used to people *telling* him what to do, what was his duty, what best for his health, his family, his land, and his people. Yet here was this soldier, not so very much older than Jack, perhaps, but with considerably more experience of the world, of commanding men in war, asking *him*... And Meade didn't even know he was the duke.

"Follow him and alert the authorities if I need to," Jack said.

"Do you need company?" Meade asked seriously. "I am happy to help."

Jack smiled. "I shan't try and fight them. I know my limitations."

"Not sure you do, old fellow." Meade raised his glass to him. "I must admit, I never expected to run into such charming people when I stumbled across this place. I even locked my door before I fell asleep in case I was robbed."

"You still might be, though I suspect Rains has enough on his plate right now. I'd lock your doors again, including cupboards." Jack had read of thieves' inns and rookeries full of secret passages and traps... And he hadn't warned Tabitha.

He rose abruptly. "I should retire and be ready for an early start."

Meade rose with him and held out his hand. "Pleasure to have made your acquaintance, sir. I hope we meet again."

"So do I," Jack said in surprise, gripping the offered hand before he went in search of someone to show him where to sleep.

Mrs. Rains did the honours somewhat ungraciously, leading him along dark and none too clean passages where cobwebs brushed his face. He caught occasional glimpses of closed doors in the solitary candle flame, and then abruptly they were at the end of the passage with a door facing them, and one on either side.

If his sense of direction had not been addled by the winding corridors, they were at the back of the house. "Where are the ladies staying?" he asked on impulse.

He more than half expected her to bridle and tell him off, and to claim, however insincerely, the respectability of the house. In his experience over the last few weeks, innkeepers were extremely careful of their reputations.

Mrs. Rains merely cackled and jerked her head at the end door facing the length of the passage, while she opened the one on the right. She walked in first and lit a solitary candle. By its light, he could make out a narrow bed with his saddle bags dumped upon it. The room smelled musty, as if it had not been slept in for years.

With a brisk nod that might have meant good night, Mrs. Rains departed, leaving him in almost total gloom. Picking up the candle holder, he went in search of another. At least the room was small, so there was not much to see except for a grubby washing bowl and a jug of cold water that might have sat there for a long time. And a cupboard door in the wall that joined with Tabitha's chamber. If he could believe Mrs. Rains.

Setting his candle down, he rummaged in his saddle bags. Over the last few weeks, he had stayed in some odd places, and he had learned the comfort and the necessity of light—something he had never even considered in his over-privileged and sheltered life. So, when he had bought his new provisions after the robbery, he had included a couple of candles. He lit one of them from the inn candle, and leaving the bedside glow he took the other light to the un-shuttered window. There were no curtains either and there was little to see outside beneath the dingy night sky.

He was completely cut off from anything that might be happening in the front inn yard. Were the Rainses merely smugglers of dubious character, or knowing traitors to their country?

Moving on from the window, he came to the cupboard. It did not have a lock, or even a bolt. He opened it, and a cobweb dropping on his face startled him. There was nothing inside the closet, but the wall was clearly much thinner here because he heard the murmur of female voices from beyond it. It seemed the ladies were not yet asleep.

He felt again the urge to tell Tabitha the truth about himself. And Lily. Whether they cared or not, it was the right thing to do. And then, if this cupboard was mirrored on their side, and there was some kind of danger from it...

He stepped inside it, gently feeling his way around its walls. The voices were much clearer here.

"How odd," Lily was saying sleepily, "that I should meet the lieutenant immediately after Ralph's betrothal story. Do you think it is fate, Tabbie?"

"No, I don't," came Tabitha's brisker tones. She forgot to drawl sometimes, perhaps when she was genuinely interested. He had won that privilege sometimes... "You will meet a great many personable young men before you need make any decision. You will most certainly not be marrying some death's head on a stick—or even on two legs—so stop worrying about it and go to sleep."

Jack stepped back as though he had been stung, his hands falling limply to his sides.

Lily giggled. "Good night, Tab."

"Good night, Lily."

Chapter Six

"**D**eath's head on a stick."

He did not know why that should hurt so much. Perhaps just because *she* said it. He had always known about the Duke of Death nickname, and to her knowledge they had never met. But was he really such a joke to society? To her?

I am not dead. In the last month, I have felt more alive than ever in my life; and in the last week...

In the last week, he had hidden and lied. Friends did not do that. Honourable men did not do that. She owed him nothing, as a stranger or as Isbourne. It mattered nothing that he was so magnanimously going to give Lily the chance to be his wife or not. He was and would always be to both of them, this pitiable laughing stock. The death's head on two ducal legs, one of which was, presumably, finely balanced on a bar of soap by the grave's edge.

He could not even laugh at himself.

At some point, he seemed to have sat down on the bed. It felt cold and faintly damp under his fingers. Nurse would be horrified. In truth, so was he, beneath the foolish humiliation of what he had overheard.

It took him some time to get all that hurt and idiocy back into proportion and remember the importance of what he had been doing in the cupboard in the first place. He had been making sure it was safe for Tabitha and Lily. That was his first priority. His second was to tell them the truth.

He got up briskly and returned to the cupboard. Though he was prepared to at least try to shut his ears, it seemed silence had fallen in the chamber next door. They must be asleep. He resumed his fingertip search around the walls.

He had just found a knobble in the wood of the ceiling, almost at the juncture with the back wall, when he heard the first swish of another movement and stilled.

It seemed to come from the other side of the cupboard wall. He held his breath, listening intently, and it came again, a definite, deliberate scratch. He placed his hand over the place the sound seemed to come from and scratched back in the same simple pattern. The scratch came again.

"Tabitha?" he whispered. "Are you in the cupboard?"

"Jack." There was amused laughter, even in her breath, and in spite of everything, it made him smile.

"I think I can make the panel open. May I try?"

There was a pause. Perhaps she was looking back at Lily in bed, or at her own *déshabillée*. In the dark cupboard, his face heated.

"Try," she whispered.

He found the knob again and pulled and pushed at it until quite suddenly, the whole back panel slid silently aside, and he was gazing at Tabitha in the candlelight. Tabitha with her luxurious hair loose about her shoulders, wearing a light dressing gown tied around the middle. She was flanked by two hanging gowns and travelling cloaks, and her cupboard door was closed.

Swallowing the sudden lump in his throat, he pointed out the knot in the ceiling and stepped back. She walked into his cupboard, and then into his chamber and closed the cupboard door.

"I don't want to wake Lily," she murmured. "But, Jack, what on earth...?"

"I think they hide in this room and use the cupboard entrance to rob the guests in the other."

"That makes alarming sense." She gazed around his room. "It explains why my room is aired and relatively clean and yours has not been touched in months. What a lucky escape to have you here."

"You were probably safe anyway tonight, what with the brandy and the Smiths. Otherwise, they would have found somewhere else to stash me."

She brushed past him and sat on the bed. "Your sheets are damp."

"I know. I intend to sleep wrapped in my coat. And hat."

Her eyes danced in the candlelight, and it felt like physical pain.

He lowered himself carefully onto the bed at a decent distance. "I need to tell you something."

"About Smith?"

"I'll follow him, make sure his presence in the country is known, along with the means."

"Is that safe?" she asked, frowning. "If he is a foreign spy... And there are three of them."

"It turns out I am good at hiding," he said ruefully. "I have not been honest with you and I want to be."

"You are going to tell me whether your name is De'Ath, or Johns, or something else altogether?"

"It's De'Ath, that much is true. John is my middle name and as a child I was known as Jack. My full name is Rudolph John De'Ath, and I am the seventh Duke of Isbourne."

Her eyes widened. She jumped to her feet, took a couple of paces toward the cupboard, and swung back before he could wipe the shame and pain from his face. Unexpectedly, she strode back and threw herself onto the bed beside him.

"You really *have* been escaping, throwing off the traces."

"I have. I had to, just once."

"Especially if you were expected to tie yourself in marriage," she said shrewdly. "Were you coming to Sark when we first met?"

"I was thinking about it, wondering if I could introduce myself as a stranger to discover the lady's true thoughts, or if I could divine them better as myself."

"And what of *your* thoughts?"

He shrugged. "If she was against it, of course I would never allow the marriage."

"And if she wasn't? If she wanted to be a duchess?"

Of course she didn't. No one wanted to be the Duchess of Death. But deliberately, he kept his face tranquil. "I will always do my duty."

She searched his eyes. "I believe you will."

"You see why I forced myself to keep my distance at the George," he said in a rush. "It was the hardest thing I ever did."

"But then, you have not been much tried, have you?"

"No," he said humbly. "But I can recognize good fortune beyond any I could ever hope for."

Her brow twitched as she continued to stare at him. In the flickering light, colour seemed to seep along the shape of her cheekbone. "Is that why you kissed me?"

"Yes," he said honestly. "I apologize if it was insulting. I did not intend that. I was only so ridiculously happy it was you."

She swung one foot back and forward as though deep in thought, but she said nothing.

"Is there a legal contract of betrothal?" he asked at last.

She shook her head. "There is an agreement of intent between her father and yours, signed long before either of you were born. Neither Lily nor I had ever heard of it before."

"Neither had I," Jack admitted.

"So why has it suddenly come to the surface now? Why is it so urgent?"

"In case I die."

Shock sprang into her eyes. "You do not appear to be at death's door to me."

"No, I am much better. Which is why my uncles seem to have decided I am fit to marry and produce heirs for Isbourne."

She was silent for a few moments, then, "Do you trust your uncles?"

"Yes."

"Really? Then why are you escaping them?"

He drew in his breath, trying to find the words for the explosion that had been building within him before he left. "I have lived with a...a surfeit of goodness."

"Smothering you," she said slowly. "Layer after layer until you can't breathe... And *they* are in control."

More than the relief of her understanding, he grasped she was speaking from her own experience. Women were subject to family control, too, and especially to a husband's. He remembered with fresh distaste that she had been married to an old man. Her surfeit was unlikely to have been of goodness.

"You are escaping, too," he blurted.

"Oh, death was kind to me," she drawled. "Now I'm looking for a purpose to it all. I'm not sure there is one. Apart from Lily."

"You are discontented."

"I am bored. Fortunately, it is fashionable."

Without intending to, he reached up and touched her cheek. "You are looking for love. I hope you find it."

For an instant she stared at him. He had the impression she was holding her breath. And then she rose fluidly to her feet and his hand fell away.

"How intriguing," she drawled, and he understood he was unbearable. "You are a romantic after all. I shan't forbid you from courting Lily, but there will be no quick marriage. As for the rest, do write and tell me if you learn anything about Smith. I shall be at Hawthorn Court for the next fortnight. After that, you may always reach me care of the Dower House at Sark Park. Good night."

He followed her, capturing her hand when it already lay on the cupboard door. She turned to face him, and he bowed over her hand to kiss it gently, to inhale the scent of her skin. When he straightened, their eyes met, and just for an instant, she looked frightened.

And then she opened the door and was gone, stepping through her own cupboard. He closed the partition by pushing the same knob inward and carefully shut the cupboard on his side.

His heart was thundering with new excitement, and his head flooded with a hundred plans, impossible, terrifying, *necessary* plans.

TABITHA DID NOT SLEEP well. She should have been angry, disgusted and insulted by Jack's deceit, but the truth was, these emotions had barely touched her. Along with a twinge of hurt, they had melted away in instinctive understanding.

In many ways, the man baffled her, but along with pity for the sickly child, so hemmed in by protectors that he had never climbed a tree or a fence, nor even been allowed to mingle with his fellow students at university, she was conscious of irritation with his guardians. How dare they impose this half-life on such a spirited person, too sweet-natured to hurt them with disobedience?

For it was not weakness. She understood that too as she lay in bed in the dark. It had taken courage to strike out alone, to find out for himself how the world worked, and what his own limits were. But there was an inner steel to him.

"If she was against it, of course I would never allow the marriage." There had been a quiet determination there, as there had been when he had refused the temptation she'd offered at the George. He did the right thing, even down to pursuing the suspicious Mr. Smith and his entourage, which was hardly the work of a duke.

She turned over again, thrusting one arm out from the covers and trying to find a cool place on the pillow.

What was it about the wretched man she found so appealing? He was certainly handsome, in a very refined kind of way, but it was the smile in his eyes that had first drawn her attention—mischievous, almost boyish, and yet with a very adult understanding. And he was attracted to her. She had always known that.

Dear God, how would she feel if Lily did marry him?

Oh, no, I am not so far gone that I cannot recover. I will be the perfect stepmother. Though I may not visit often...

She felt again the lingering caress of his lips on her hand. So distant a kiss should not set her pulses racing, though there might have been an excuse outside when he had kissed her mouth with such unexpected if all too brief firmness. He would be such a wonderful lover, tender, attentive, with his long, slender body that would look so beautiful naked, and feel so good in her arms. No rough, drunken fumbling for quick gratification or domination...

She yanked the pillow over her face and pushed it away again. He was right. She had been searching for love. That was the meaning she had sought after Sark's death had finally freed her from the horrors of marriage. No one since had been so cruel to her. They had all been flatteringly avid and grateful, but each of her three illicit lovers had disappointed her. There had been no love in the loving. A transient half-pleasure did not outweigh her sense of regret, and she had almost decided to stop looking.

It would be the same with him. *I am seeking something that does not exist.*

He would be kind to Lily. There was nothing of the "death's head" or even the invalid about him. The girl could do worse, much worse, than be the Duchess of Isbourne.

And like him, Tabitha would do her duty, watch him grow to love Lily as he might have loved her...

She threw herself onto her back, listening to the creaking joints of the old house. At some point, just as the early summer dawn was breaking, she heard several equine snorts outside, and the slow, gentle thud of many hooves, as though several ponies were wearing stockings as they were led away from the inn.

Was the contraband all hidden now? Would Smith vanish silently during the night with the ponies, or move openly on his way, wherever that was, in full daylight?

She worried for Jack's safety—the duke's safety—but curiously she found she did not fear for *him*. He would find a way to deal with any situations that arose.

She just wished she were going with him. And the intensity of that longing did shock her.

SHE AND LILY ROSE AS soon as the inn began to stir, and it seemed all the guests at the Headless Horse had the same idea. Everyone who had been present last night was again in the common room, although this time, fraternization was kept to a minimum.

The Smiths sat where they had on the previous evening, wading through what seemed to be a fried version of last night's mutton stew. At quite the other end of the room, Lieutenant Meade and Jack sat at separate tables, each set for one.

All the men rose and bowed at Tabitha's amused "Good morning." She managed not to look at Jack and was glad to be distracted by an entirely different maid coming to greet them and inviting them to the last available table between Jack and Meade.

By the time Tabitha had asked for tea and toast, the Frenchmen—if they were French —were making their exit, with polite farewells. The guests left behind exchanged glances. Almost immediately, the sounds of trotting hooves in the yard told Tabitha the Smiths' mounts had already been saddled and waiting.

No one spoke. Jack gazed into his cup until the sound of the hooves had faded.

"Such an early start puts the rest of us to shame," he said, finishing whatever was in his cup and rising to his feet. "I too must be off. Ladies, your servant. Meade, farewell and good luck."

He picked his saddle bags off the floor beside his table and sauntered off. Would he even be able to tell which direction the Smiths had taken? At the door he paused and glanced back directly at Tabitha. A quick, fugitive smile flickered, and her heart turned over. She could not help smiling back.

And then he was gone. No saddled horse awaited him, judging by the quiet that followed.

Lieutenant Meade said diffidently, "Since our destination is the same, may I escort you, ladies?"

Beneath the table, Lily's foot pressed on Tabitha's. Well, it was one way of getting to know the young man, and since the outriders were with the baggage coach, an extra man might well prove useful.

"How very kind," Tabitha said affably.

They saw no sign of their hosts as they paid their shot to the maid and departed. No doubt their late night had caught up with them. James the coachman certainly had nothing good to say about the house.

"Slap-dash care for the horses—had to do most of it meself. And a racket going on all night. They're up to no good, my lady, mark my words. Shouldn't even be stopping at a place like this never mind staying the night. I'm only surprised you weren't robbed blind."

"Well, I own I'm grateful that we had nothing of value with us. But take heart, James, we have survived. On to Hawthorn Court. Lieutenant Meade here will accompany us."

James gave him the usual sharp-eyed stare but made no objection.

The journey, remarkably easy in the daylight, passed pleasantly enough. Tabitha even nodded off at one point, soothed by the chatter of the younger people.

It was just after midday when Lady Hawthorn welcomed them with literally open arms. In fact, she was so genuinely delighted that Tabitha remembered all over again why she was so fond of her friend.

She drew Lily forward, "Louisa, this is my stepdaughter, Lady Lily Lisle. Lily, Lady Hawthorn, your kind hostess."

Lily curtseyed gracefully. "It was so very kind of your ladyship to invite me, especially when I am not quite *out*."

"My, you are so pretty you will break hearts! You are very welcome, my dear. How ridiculous, Tabitha, that you should have a grown-up daughter!"

"There are less than seven years between us," Lily confided.

"But I am still the strictest of chaperones," Tabitha said lightly. She knew Louisa Hawthorn would accept that as the warning it was, pass it on to those most likely to try to overstep, and keep her own watch as hostess. "Oh, and I believe you know Lieutenant Meade, who has been gracious enough to escort us on the last stage of our journey."

"Why, Nat, I would never have known you," Louisa exclaimed. "What a fine officer you make! You must know that your family has been prostrate with worry since you did not arrive yesterday evening." She swung on her butler who was standing patiently to one side. "Chivers, send word to Mrs. Meade that the lieutenant has arrived, and take him up to his room. Make yourself at home, Nat, and do join us in the garden whenever you wish. Tea is at four... Come Tabbie, I have the perfect rooms set aside for you. Your bags are already unpacked, of course, since your woman arrived with them yesterday..."

Tabitha saw at once why her old friend described the rooms as perfect for her. She had said that she would rather share with Lily than have the girl any further away than next door, when it was her first ever house party. Louisa had done better. She had given them rooms with a connecting door, a lockable door at that from Tabitha's side. As if she would indulge in any affairs, discreet or otherwise, with Lily under the same roof!

For no clear reason, Jack popped into her mind. He had been doing so all day at both convenient and inconvenient moments.

"How lovely," Tabitha said hastily, admiring the tasteful wallpaper, picked out in blue to match the hangings. Lily's room was decorated in palest pink.

"Then I'll leave you to settle in. You have a view of the garden Tab. Do feel free to wander down whenever you like. Today, everything is informal since people are still arriving at all sorts of odd hours..."

She fluttered off, clearly enjoying the sheer busy-ness of her first ever house party.

Lily came dancing through the open connecting door. "My room is delightful! Perfectly charming. But so is yours. Everything looks so smart and new compared to Sark Park. Do you think Ralph is a penny-pincher?"

"Either by inclination or necessity. Let us not think of him when we are here to enjoy ourselves."

Tabitha lay down on the bed and stretched luxuriously, but any intentions she might have harboured of indulging in a short, reviving nap, were thwarted almost at once by a knock on the bedchamber door.

Sighing, Tabitha sat up and climbed off the bed. "Come in."

The door flew open and her brother Barty sauntered in, grinning. "Well met, Tabs!" he said carelessly before his eyes widened as he noticed Lily. "Greetings, Squib, *you* brush up pretty well, don't you?"

Lily laughed but repressed her usual retort to Barty's teasing since someone else had followed him into the room. With annoyance, Tabitha saw that it was Lord Carily, who had pursued her in Brighton. She had considered being caught, for he was an attractive man and entertaining, but she had chosen to leave the town for Sark Park and keep her appointment with Lily.

"My lord," she said distantly. "I did not expect your presence here."

"Fortunately, fair Lady Hawthorn was won over by my charms," Carily said winningly. "Or at least, she took pity on me languishing in the outer darkness of separation from you."

"Well, languish elsewhere," she said, making shooing motions with her hands. "Barty, my bedchamber is not a salon for meetings of your friends. Go away."

"Fair enough," said Barty, who clearly had no real desire to be there.

"But cruel," Carily complained, clutching his heart as though wounded. "If I may not stay, at least come and walk with me in the garden."

"No," Tabitha said bluntly.

Barty was already opening the door while Carily tried to stare Tabitha down. She sighed wearily, and a hint of colour seeped into his face. At last he turned smartly and followed Barty from the room.

I do hope you are not going to be troublesome...

Chapter Seven

At Sark Park, Ralph, acknowledged as the earl by almost everyone, paced his study. At least, he called it his study and tried desperately to think of it as his own, but in truth it still smelled of his uncle Althorpe. It was full of his uncle's old-fashioned furniture and tobacco-stained walls, hung with his uncle's taste in pictures—hunting and banqueting scenes. And even the books old Sark had kept here, calling them too artistic for feminine eyes, were somewhat coarsely illustrated examples of plain vulgarity and not remotely to his taste. He was sure Portia had discovered them, for she abetted his efforts to keep the children out of the room. Which was useful when Ralph needed to think.

As he paced, he was manufacturing a false crisis in his mind that would be guaranteed to bring Lily home while leaving Tabitha well out of the way at Hawthorn Court. Lord Hazlett's last letter had stated that his grace was travelling by easy stages and would no doubt write before he arrived, which made his visit sound imminent. And Lily, such a pretty little thing, would surely be irresistible, particularly to a man starved of female companionship. By then, the young idiot would be desperate to give away wealth he would hardly miss, without paying too much attention as to exactly where it was going.

Then, whatever happened, even if the worst came to the worst, he would be safe. It remained a capital plan, if only Tabitha could be prevented from interfering. Considering Sark had abused and bullied the woman for the entire five years of their marriage, it was utterly ridiculous and yet oh so typical of the man that his one sign of respect to his last wife was to give her control of Ralph's one immediate asset. Lily.

A knock interrupted his tortuous calculations, and he scowled at the footman who entered.

"My lord, a gentleman has called asking for a moment of your time."

The duke so filled his thoughts that he jumped to an immediate conclusion without pausing to think that the duke had neither written in advance nor sent in his card. Ralph's scowl melted.

"Show him in, Joseph, show him in!"

Ralph straightened his cravat where he had tugged at it absently and brushed down his coat. Anxiously, he eyed the decanters on the side cabinet. There was enough in each for a glass, though an invalid might well prefer tea...

"Mr. Smith," Joseph announced, inexplicably, and a man older than himself walked into the room.

Even the sickest twenty-year-old could not look thirty years older. Ralph felt his welcoming smile fade and strove to hold it in place as the stranger bowed.

"I hope you will forgive the intrusion," Mr. Smith said in the accents of a gentleman. "But I thought it best to come to you first, both to apologize for my tardiness, and to give you fair warning before the scandal sheets get hold of the story, as they inevitably will."

"What story?" Ralph asked blankly.

"Perhaps you had better sit down."

Ralph raised his eyebrows. "My good sir, don't you feel it is a little impertinent for you to invite me to sit?"

Smith smiled ruefully. "Actually, no. I'm afraid that I gave your servants a false name in order to avoid gossip at this point. My name is Hunter Lisle and I am afraid, to put it in a nutshell, sir, this is not your house."

Ralph stepped back toward the bell pull, saying haughtily. "I have the name and pedigree that says it is."

"So do I," Smith said, and Ralph's hand paused in mid-air. "And it is a fact that mine trumps yours. Being the son of the third earl's second son, and you the son of his third."

"But...Carrington is dead! There were no children."

"I beg to differ," Smith said gently. "I am, you see, very much alive." Smith held out his hand. "Cousin Ralph."

Ralph stared at the hand in loathing, and his false cousin let it fall back to his side. This was why the Writ of Summons was taking so long. This imposter had delayed it.

"I wrote from Canada some months ago," the imposter said. "Did you not receive my letter?"

"I put it in the fire with other rubbish and begging letters."

"I'm afraid this is a shock to you."

"Not at all." Ralph yanked the bell rope and for once Joseph appeared almost immediately. Ralph hoped he had not been listening at the door. "Mr. Smith is leaving. Show him out."

JACK WAS RESTING HIS new horse at the side of the road, within sight of the Sark Park gates. It had taken him several changes of horses to keep up with the Smiths, but somehow he had never suspected they were coming here.

Could the new Earl of Sark be somehow involved in this smuggling of French people? If Tabitha's cousin by marriage was a traitor, it put a whole new complexion upon everything. Jack's aim had not changed, but discretion might well be called for, since he could not bear Tabitha to suffer from this.

Long before he had expected it, the three horsemen walked their mounts out of the gate and turned right toward the London road.

Confused, Jack followed on and realized, eventually, that his quarries were indeed heading toward the capital. He didn't follow too closely, instead preferring to ask for them at the posting inns along the way.

The closer he drew to London, the more uneasy he got. Uncle Ha-zlett was always in Town when he was not at Isley, and the other uncles were also frequent visitors. In addition, several of his doctors lived there, and when London was thin of company, he was more likely to stand out.

And yet, he needed to follow Smith. He never thought seriously about giving up, but gradually, following his quarries more closely through the tollgates into the city, several plans began to converge in his mind. They thrummed excitingly in the background while he strove to keep his quarries in sight.

It would be easy to lose oneself in the heaving melting pot of people that made up London. He almost expected the Smiths to dive into the back streets to do just that. Instead, they went quite openly and directly to Albemarle Street and Grillon's Hotel. As if they knew the way.

Well, it was easy enough to keep maps in one's head. Jack was doing much the same, for although he had made occasional trips to London with his guardians, he did not know the city well. Somewhere close to the hotel was Isbourne House, his town residence, though he could count on one hand the number of nights he had stayed there. A spurt of curiosity struck him, but he ignored it, preferring to watch the hotel door. Smith and his son went inside, leaving the servant with the horses.

Jack dismounted, inspecting his tired horse as though worried about it while he watched for the Smiths' exit. Ostlers appeared and led the horses away. The servant followed them. It seemed they were putting up at Grillon's.

Jack was just beginning to feel conspicuous, when Smith emerged again alone and spoke to the doorman, who immediately summoned a waiting hackney carriage. Alarmed that he might lose his quarry, Jack led his horse nearer, but he was not quick enough to hear the direction to the jarvey.

Instead, as the hackney horses trotted off, he addressed the doorman, "The devil, I've missed him," he said in annoyed tones. "Was that not Mr. Smith?"

"No, sir," said the well-trained doorman, who would not give away the names of residents to strangers. However, the tiniest trace of relief in the man's face told Jack he was not lying because he didn't need to. Mr. Smith had changed his name.

Jack swung himself into the saddle and trotted off in pursuit of the hackney—no easy task in the chaotic, snarling mess of carriages, carts, drays, and pedestrians in Piccadilly. Several times, he was sure he had lost the hackney in the host of other vehicles. Once he almost followed a different carriage, only to discover the grey horse that had been his guide trotting along beside him. He dared not look inside the carriage.

Oddly, Smith was travelling toward the city, where Jack had been before with Uncle Hazlett. Finally, the hackney stopped and Smith got out. The hackney waited.

Again, Jack dismounted and led his horse past the nameplate on the door. Turnbull, Turnbull & Vernon, Solicitors. Interesting. He moved on, as though searching for a different office, as indeed he was. Only two doorways further on, he found the office of the De'Ath family solicitors, Langham, Fortnum and Dabbs.

Jack hesitated, for there were matters he needed to discuss with them. But he wasn't yet sure he wanted word of his presence getting back to the uncles, and in any case, he needed to know what Smith was doing. Calling on a reputable solicitor was hardly the act of an enemy spy smuggled into the country with illicit brandy.

In fact, Smith spent so long inside that Jack began to wonder if he had been given the slip. Then, as he walked past the door yet again, he almost bumped into Smith emerging precipitously from the doorway. They both murmured apologies without looking at each other, and Smith reached for the hackney door.

"Back to Grillon's," he instructed.

There was no urgency about following him there. In fact, consulting his fob watch, Jack came to a sudden decision and sought out lodgings for himself and his horse. Having unpacked his saddle bags in an indifferent room of a backstreet inn close to Grillon's, he sat down at the rickety table and wrote several letters. Then, although it was getting a little late, he went in search of his tailor.

His escape had been fun. Also enlightening and helpful and utterly life-changing. But it was time to stop hiding and face that life on his own terms. And somehow, that was more exciting than almost anything else.

PART OF JACK'S MAJOR decision was the acknowledgement that he was quite out of his depth with the Smith business, and it was too important, too dangerous to the country, for him to blunder about with it any further. He had resolved to lay the whole matter before a magistrate and let the law investigate and involve any government departments it needed to.

On his way to Bow Street, however, he called in at several shops, and then the offices of Langham, Fortnum and Dabbs, the De'Ath solicitors, where he had a long discussion with Mr. Langham. The elderly lawyer clarified exactly where Jack stood in terms of the trust, his guardians, and the betrothal agreement between his father and the late Lord Sark.

In fact, Mr. Langham showed him the original document signed by the two men. "In my opinion, it is unenforceable, nothing more than a fond parental wish. Whether your grace considers it a matter of private honour, is not for me to say." He set the document aside. "Now, as to funds while you are in London, I shall give you a letter of introduction to the manager of the bank, since you have not previously met."

This was something of a relief to Jack, who had begun to run short of money.

"Isbourne House is shut up, as you know, but it can be made comfortable for you within a few days."

"Ah, that won't be necessary on this occasion, since I aim to leave London tomorrow."

"Very well. Um..." For the first time, Langham looked awkward, shuffling documents on his desk and shifting in his chair. He pulled his lower lip between his teeth. "Perhaps you are not aware that Lord Hazlett wrote to me, asking if you had visited me. He seemed genuinely anxious for your welfare."

"I have written to him, so feel free to disclose my visit."

Langham's gaze, over the top of his half-spectacles, was perceptive. "Sometimes one needs to escape in order to appreciate home. Will you be seeing your physician while you are in town?"

Jack smiled. "No. I appear to have no need of him." He rose to his feet and offered his hand. "Thank you for all your help, Mr. Langham."

The lawyer shook hands with surprising warmth. "My pleasure, your grace."

His head spinning, Jack stepped out into the street and halted to adjust his mind to the next matter. The street was busy with scurrying, respectably dressed men, a few passing carriages, and a crossing sweeper. A hackney had stopped at the side of the road, and its horse pawed the ground impatiently, while it's driver, down from his box, was patting the animal's neck in sympathy. It was too hot.

Smith. Bow Street.

Jack's neck prickled. He turned to the right and looked straight into the eyes of Smith himself.

The man must have just emerged from his own solicitor's office and was striding straight toward him.

In the same instant, Smith clearly recognized Jack, for his eyes widened in surprise and he came to a sudden halt a couple of feet away. "Mr. Johns!"

"Mr. Smith. What a small -"

A sudden loud crack broke through the buzz of the bustling street, making several people start and even cry out, looking wildly around. Mr. Smith, in the midst of a hasty step closer to Jack, jerked his arm as though surprised.

At the side window of the hackney, a curtain swished, catching Jack's eye. He glanced back at Smith, a question ready on his lips. He never spoke it, for a dark, red stain was blooming on the sleeve of Smith's coat.

"Dear God." Jack took the man by the good arm. "You've been—"

"Don't make a fuss," Smith said. "I suspect it's a mere graze."

Quite suddenly, Jack grasped several things, the most important of which was that Smith had been shot from the window of the waiting hackney. And it could happen again. Instinctively, Jack stepped between Smith and the carriage.

"He's leaving," Smith said, "by the other door... I don't feel in a position to chase him right now. I wouldn't mind so much, but that's *my* blessed hackney."

Supporting Smith toward it, Jack wrenched open the door and, finding it empty, helped the now white-faced injured man inside.

"Grillon's," Jack snapped at the jarvey, who left off gawping at the passers-by now gathered in huddles to discuss what on earth had happened, and lumbered hastily toward his box.

Jack leapt inside the carriage and closed the door, searching out of all the windows for any threats, before dropping onto the bench beside Smith. He helped him off with his coat, and Smith slashed the sleeve of his shirt with his own pocket knife, then used the hacked-off material to wipe the blood from his arm.

"Yes, it just grazed me," Smith said with some satisfaction. "I must have moved just at the wrong moment for him. Or you did and distracted his aim."

"But who would be shooting at you in such a way?" Jack asked grimly. "In the middle of the city! This makes no sense." Unless it was some secret British attempt at assassinating a spy... Was he naïve to imagine his country would not behave in such an underhand manner? Only, how would they know?

"You think I have not been in England long enough to make enemies?" Smith asked sardonically.

"Allow me," Jack said, taking the torn sleeve from him and making a proper pad which he tied over the wound using his own handkerchief.

"How did you know I was staying at Grillon's?" Smith asked.

Jack glanced at him. He showed no sign of pain. His eyes were hard, but direct, curiously honest.

"I followed you there yesterday," Jack said evenly. "Considering how you arrived in this country and the fluency of your French, I was suspicious."

Smith's lips quirked. "Many people in Canada speak French, you know. After thirty years there, I *should* be fluent."

Jack helped him back into his coat. "Yes, but should your ship be blown so badly off course that it was wrecked off Brittany?"

"No. That was damnable luck, and I confess I thought we were done for. But our—er...fluency got us out of that scrape and into another with my friends the smugglers."

Jack frowned. "Then your ridiculous story is actually true?"

"Sadly, yes. An adventure to entertain my grandchildren, should I ever have any."

Jack was slowly adjusting. "Why do I believe you now when I could swear you were lying at the Headless Horseman?"

"I *was* lying at the Headless Horseman. Not about my journey, but about my name, which is not Smith. In retrospect, that was a poor lie, but I didn't expect to be asked by anyone who cared about the answer. I own my name is not Smith. It is Lisle. Hunter Lisle, and I am the true Earl of Sark. I trust that does not make us enemies?"

"Not without some considerable hypocrisy on my part," Jack said. "For my name isn't Johns either. It's Rudolph John De'Ath, and I am the Duke of Isbourne."

Smith stared at him, and then slowly, his eyes began to laugh. "I like you, Rudolph John De'Ath! Come and meet my son, and together we shall form our own Society of the Noble *Incogniti*."

HALF AN HOUR LATER, with Lisle's wound properly tended by his silent servant, and over a pleasant luncheon with the father and son, Jack heard the whole tale.

"My father, Carrington Lisle, never expected to be earl. In fact, he quarrelled with his whole family and hated both his brothers, so he went adventuring on his own account, and ended up in Canada, where I was born. My mother was a Frenchwoman, which is another reason the language comes easily to both my son Edward and me. We had cut all ties with the other Lisles long ago, but we still received occasional letters from solicitors in England, informing us of various deaths, including that of my uncle Althorpe, Earl of Sark.

"Oddly enough, I didn't think anything of it until my wife died a month later, and I began to question everything. I was restless. And it suddenly struck me that if Sark had no direct heirs, as the solicitor had informed me, then I was the next in line for the earldom. It made me laugh, until I realized I had no right to keep such an opportunity from Edward. Then another letter from the solicitor informed me inquiries were being made by the Lord Chancelor's office into the issue of Carrington Lisle, my father. Edward and I talked about it and decided to go to England and see how we liked it.

"Perhaps it was a poor decision, considering the wide range of the war with France, and then the outbreak of another with the United States, but as I say, it was an adventure..."

He reached for the wine bottle and refilled Jack's glass. "My father spoke of the old country sometimes. About growing up at Sark Park. But I hadn't expected to feel anything for it. I never feel for places, only people. Yet there was something about landing in England, even in such a way. And Sark..."

He cast an apologetic smile at Jack. "I liked it. Edward liked it. Even so, we would have simply vanished again, gone back to Canada or somewhere entirely new, but I went to talk to my cousin who is installed there and calling himself earl. The house is frankly tatty. The servants, the tenants, and labourers are all poor. The place is run into the ground. And according to the solicitor, Ralph, like old Sark, is ignoring all advice in favour of short-term gain. He is a terrible steward of the land, and I could do better for everyone. Actually, my dog could."

He twisted the stem of his glass and set it down on the table. "So I presented the solicitor with proof of my identity and explained my somewhat unconventional entry into the country. He is sorting it all out and will pass my documents along to the Lord Chancelor. Although, of course, you are welcome to make your own inquiries. I'll even give you a letter."

Jack felt his face heat. "I'm afraid I was living my own version of a school boy's tale of spies and traitors. You have nothing to prove to me. Are you aware there is a plan afoot to marry old Sark's youngest daughter to me?"

"Is there? I suppose you are rich? Then you are to supply the money to keep Ralph's creditors at bay and allow his family to live in luxury—less tatty luxury than now. Do you want the marriage?"

"That is for the future," Jack said evasively, "but I don't know where Ralph got the idea that either my uncles or I are quite so easy to touch."

"I expect he has not met you," Lisle said wryly.

"I'm not sure anyone has." *Except Tabitha...* He blinked suddenly. "Ralph is your enemy... *Ralph* tried to shoot you?"

"Or he sent someone. No one else has a cause to, and Ralph is a desperate man. I could see he liked his dignity and it is, frankly, easier to live on tick with a title. I am endangering everything by disputing the title, including this marriage contract. *Are* you likely to withdraw from the offer?"

"I haven't made any offer, but I take your point. If you had left it another month, he thinks he would have tricked a fortune out of me. But here you are threatening to kick him out of both the earldom *and* the fortune."

"Will he try again, Papa?" Edward asked, looking rather pale.

"Actually, I'm not sure he will," Jack said, thinking about it. "He took an awful risk. Don't you think it was sheer impulse? I expect he was merely visiting his solicitor and saw you going in ahead of him. So he waited. And when the jarvey climbed down, he took the opportunity to slip into the hackney."

Jack threw down his fork and sat back, frowning. "Except he already had the gun with him. Who carries a firearm to call on their lawyer?"

"You'd be surprised," Lisle said ruefully. "In fact, I suspect the pistol was mine. Old habits die hard. I took it out of my document case and left it in the hackney, since it was ordered to wait for me. He must have found it there. It was certainly gone when I returned with your help."

"So, the chances are, he doesn't know you're at Grillon's," Jack said uneasily. "Is that good enough? He has to be warned off—and the only way to do that is to publicize your claim to the earldom immediately. Then any attack on you will be laid at his door. Write him a formal letter, copied to your solicitor. Talk about it loudly in public and slip a word to the press. Start calling yourself Lord Sark while the lawyers fight it out."

Smith grinned and raised his glass to him. "You are very wise for one so young."

THE FOLLOWING MORNING, to the blare of news sheet sellers and running patterers shouting about the new earl back from the dead, Jack packed his new coats, shirts, and undergarments in his new bags and supervised their bestowal in his hired post-chaise. He paid his shot, tipped the staff, and climbed into the chaise like the Duke of Isbourne, not the Duke of Death.

He was smiling, his heart beating with excitement as he laid his new, curly-brimmed beaver hat on the seat beside him and watched the grimy, vital streets of London slip past. He was the duke, and he was going home. Just not yet.

Chapter Eight

Master George Hawthorn climbed over the steep side of his cot, landed on the nursery floor, and grabbed hold of Tabitha's skirts to steady himself. He grinned up at her with such a wealth of pride and mischief that she laughed.

"Don't encourage him," begged his mother. "How are we to keep him safe when he can do that?"

Tabitha ruffled the child's fair, tousled head. There was an odd ache behind her amusement. "That's why you have a nursery maid."

"Even nursery maids have to sleep sometimes," Louisa said.

"Fortunately, so do children. Or so I'm told."

Little George wrapped his arms around his mother's legs and she bent and lifted him into her arms. "You, my little man, are a large sack of trouble. What are you?"

"Large sack of trouble," George said obligingly and pressed his cheek to his mother's, his fat little arms around her neck.

She laughed, kissed him, and deposited him on the floor. "Go to Kitty, then, and Papa will come and see you shortly."

Tabitha led the way out of the nursery, surprised by her own reluctance. She rather liked George. Not that Louisa's party was dull. She had enjoyed a treasure hunt and an excursion to the local castle ruins, amateur dramatic practice and a tea dance. On top of which, some of the company was witty, and Lily was proving quite a success. She behaved well in company, managing an excellent balance between lively and natural on one side, and modest and polite on the other. Tabitha was proud of her.

The girl had many admirers, of course, and she was careful not to favour one over the others. But there was a special warmth in her eyes whenever they landed on Lieutenant Meade.

"Another fine afternoon for tea in the garden," Tabitha remarked.

"And opportunities for quiet walks in the gardens," Louisa said, nudging her elbow lightly. "Carily seems to be growing quite desperate."

"He is certainly growing confoundedly dull."

Louisa blinked. "Truly? But I thought you liked him! You did in Brighton."

"On closer acquaintance, I was mistaken."

"Are you just saying that because of Lily's presence? There are discreet ways to meet, you know. But in truth, Tabbie, I think he is serious. He would marry you in a trice and it is a good match."

"Good God, no. It took me five years to be rid of my last husband. I am not about to be trapped with another."

Louisa could not help giggling in a shocked kind of way. "You do say the most outrageous things! Carily is nothing like Sark, and marriage need not be a prison."

Tabitha patted her arm. "You are very lucky with Sir Peter, and I am happy for you, but marriage does not suit me. In fact, I'm not sure I don't prefer celibacy. I shall retire to my dower estate and breed pugs."

"Pugs? Seriously?"

"Seriously. They are such amusing little creatures and so affectionate. Loyal too. Why would I need a man?"

Louisa took her arm cozily. "*Well*, my dear, if you don't know..."

"Stop," Tabitha said as they strolled out into the garden, "I aspire to *utter* respectability."

"Ha," said her hostess rudely. "Go on without me. I hear Chivers in the hall..."

Tabitha discovered Lily seated informally with some other young people on a rug spread over the lawn. Meade was among them, but fortunately Carily was not.

"Tabbie!" Lily greeted her. "You must join our team—you are the best at pall-mall."

Tabitha lowered herself among them. "I'm not, you know."

Before the inevitable chivalrous arguments could arise and bore her, Lord Durward strolled over, surrounded by his usual aura of recklessness and danger. He was the surprise attendee at the party, for he was rumoured to have fled the country to avoid retribution for his latest duel. He had arrived at Hawthorn Court only yesterday, several days late, and caused a ripple of eager interest.

Tabitha had no chance to speak to him before and was not really in any hurry to introduce him to Lily, for his danger lay as much in his charm as in his temper. In fact, Tabitha rather liked him and was, indeed, on terms of friendly flirtation with him.

Lounging at her side, he presented her with a daisy chain. "Accept my humble offering, Lady Sark."

"Gratefully," Tabitha responded, placing the circle on her hair at a rakish angle. "Just what my ensemble needed. How are you, Durward? I thought you were abroad."

"Skulked in Harwich for a week or so with that aim, fell badly in love with a tug-boat captain's daughter, and strove to mend my ways. Then I heard Foster was sitting up in bed, bright as a button, and I was unlikely to be had up for murder after all. Naturally, I could not resist Lady H's gathering." He smiled into her eyes. "Especially as I knew *you* would be present."

"How gratifying to be recalled in the same breath as the tug-boat captain's daughter. But I'm glad about Foster."

"Me too," Durward said, and for an instant, there was rueful fervour in his voice that provided some hope he would give up his appalling habit of duelling. The near death of his last opponent seemed to have given him a much-needed fright. "Won't you introduce me?"

There was a distinct flutter among Lily's friends, including the very young men who were quite in awe of the notorious Durward. Several chaperones moved nearer and sat down at the closest garden table to protect their charges.

Only Lieutenant Meade seemed unaware of the Foster *on-dit*.

"Who is Foster and what did you do?" he asked bluntly.

"Can't say in front of the ladies," Durward replied. "An unedifying tale of idiocy and remorse. Hello, what's got Carily so puffed-up?"

Carily was indeed strutting across the lawn like a bird showing off his plumage, but he was also clearly big with news, as the saying went. His bright blue eyes positively gleamed as he swerved toward Tabitha's group.

"Out with it, Carily," said Durward. "Unless it's too scandalous for company."

"Don't be an ass, Durward, how would *you* know if it was?" He grinned to the company in general, and then, more broadly, to Tabitha. "You'll never guess who is with Lady H."

"You are right," Tabitha murmured.

"Who?" asked Lily naively.

"The Duke of Death."

It was so totally unexpected that Tabitha's stomach bumped. Lily paled.

"He isn't real," Lily's new friend, Amelia scoffed.

"Of course he is real," Barty said. "I saw him at Oxford once."

"So did I," Durward said. "The year I left."

"Is he in a bath chair?" someone asked.

"No, on his legs," said Carily, grinning, "although a puff of breeze through the closing front door did almost blow him over."

"What on earth brings him here?" Miss Saunders wondered. She carried with her the superior confidence of a successful Season in London. "Surely Lady Hawthorn did not invite him? None of the hostesses do so anymore because he never comes and no one has ever met him anyway."

Lily was gazing at Tabitha, her eyes stricken.

"It makes no difference," Tabitha said to her, which had the effect of soothing Lily and baffling the others. "His grace is Lady Hawthorn's guest," she said vaguely.

"Is he staying, then?" Lily's friend Amelia asked eagerly. After all, an unmarried duke at the party raised the stakes for everyone, but particularly those in the marriage mart.

"I have absolutely no idea," Tabitha said, just as Louisa led a gentleman out of the French window onto the lawn.

A ripple of excitement was spreading around the garden, via the listening dowagers and those who had overheard Carily's announcement. All eyes had turned on the two figures strolling out into the garden, some more surreptitiously than others. The commotion was subtle but definite, as mamas positioned their daughters to attract attention either by walking in the duke's path, or sitting at a table with an invitingly free chair beside it. A buzz of conversation swelled, like an approaching swarm of bees.

Tabitha did not watch the progress. She made some remark to one of the chaperones, which began a trivial conversation in which she had no interest, while her mind spun a whole web of questions. Why had he come? Could it possibly be for her? Had he missed her, or solved the mystery of Smith and decided to keep his word about telling her?

Or had he come for Lily? God knew that was the likeliest answer. He was doing the right thing, and he would find her at her best. Whether Lily would forgive him his deception or not was another matter, for Tabitha had told her nothing about her late-night conversation at the Headless Horseman.

"Come on Durward," Carily said, grinning as he rose gracefully to his feet. "Let's blow the reed over."

"Not I," Durward said lazily. "Always curious to meet a living legend."

"Only just living," Carily drawled.

One of the younger men chuckled and rose with him, attracted, no doubt, by the atmosphere of a schoolboy prank. And Tabitha suddenly panicked for Jack, who had never been to school, had known only a very sheltered version of university life, and was entirely unused to society of this kind, to snakes like Carily.

She did not even question her suddenly clear opinion of Carily. He had always been a snake. He even moved like one. She just hadn't cared until now when he could surely destroy Jack's social credibility and any burgeoning self-confidence. The urge to protect him took her by surprise.

At least Louisa was bringing him this way. At last, she turned her head and her breath vanished.

There was no sign of the diffident young duke, escaping undue attention in worn riding dress. Just for an instant, she even thought it was not Jack at all, but some imposter, or Jack had lied to her about that too.

But no, these were Jack's refined, almost delicate features, his pale face and his smooth black hair, although it had been cut into a smarter style. His slight frame was encased in a superbly cut blue coat and elegant pantaloons, perfect for afternoon visiting. His cravat was snowy white and well if plainly tied, fastened with a simple gold pin. And he was not even looking at her.

His eyes cold and indifferent like the rest of his face, he gazed around the garden or upon his hostess whenever they spoke.

Lily said, "But that's..."

Tabitha leaned into her, digging with her elbow, and Lily trailed into silence. Fortunately, everyone else's attention was on the duke, because Louisa, as Tabitha's friend, had brought him to meet her first.

"Goodness, so many introductions to make!" Louisa said, coming to a halt between the chaperones' table and the young people's blanket. "Your grace, allow me to present Lady Sark."

Durward and the other remaining young man had risen to their feet, but the duke's uninterested gaze focused briefly on Tabitha without recognition or warmth. He bowed very slightly from the waist, and Tabitha inclined her head. She felt stiff and...and *hurt*.

His cool gaze moved on as he acknowledged each of Louisa's introductions in the same manner.

"The Duke of Isbourne," she finished, rather like a conjurer at a fair. "He bears a message to you, Tab, from someone called Sir Hubert, but I am trying to persuade him to join our little party. Tea will be served any moment. Do sit down, your grace..."

She flitted off, taking an unnecessarily circuitous route back to the house, no doubt to spread the gossip of the duke's arrival as she went.

The duke sat down in the vacant chair at the chaperone's table.

Tabitha, for once, could think of nothing to say. Had he really brought a message from the magistrate whom she had told about the highwayman? Or was that a mere excuse to see her? Or Lily?

"Very pleased to meet your grace finally," Durward said in his easy manner. "I have always accounted myself indebted to you for the princely sum of five guineas which I won in a wager at Oxford."

The duke's expressionless lips parted. "Over whether or not I would die there?"

Only Durward seemed immune from the chill shock of that. "Oh no, whether or not you were there at all! I glimpsed you through a guard of prissy old bores on Magdalen Bridge."

Everyone seemed to hold their collective breath, waiting for his haughty grace to take offence. Behind Jack's chair, Carily and his acolyte strolled past, blowing at the back of the ducal head. One of the youths on the blanket giggled.

Jack's gaze met Durward's. His lip twitched. "That would have been me," he allowed. "Though I confess I do not recall you."

"No reason why you should. You can't have been there long, and I was in my final year."

"We must have been in the same year," Barty remarked. "I remember you too."

"I'm only sorry we were not acquainted at the time," the duke said graciously. Behind him, Carily and his friend, strolled past once more, closer this time, blowing audibly this time and creasing up with laughter. Everyone pretended not to see them, though Tabitha felt her lips tighten. "Does anyone else feel the draught of hot air?"

Tabitha laughed, and Carily coloured angrily to have been so neatly and so unanswerably reduced. Durward grinned at the duke, and the young girls looked bewildered, though Lily was frowning.

Perhaps Jack could deal with society's snakes after all. He seemed to have judged to a nicety just how far to let Carily go without making fuss or complaint. She could almost see those who were nearby adjusting their opinions and expectations. Amelia gazed at him with new interest and Miss Saunders put on her best, sophisticated smile.

Tabitha glanced at the duke once more, and found his gaze on her face, still cool, still expressionless.

"Perhaps, Lady Sark, you will allow me to discharge my duty by Sir Hubert?"

"Of course," she said, allowing only the faintest hint of curiosity into her voice. She waited.

"Then do accompany me to the arbour before tea is served." He rose, moved toward her and even held down his hand to help her rise.

It was an oddly commanding gesture, which inevitably set her back up. On the other hand, she needed to know what he was up to. The faintest twitch of his brow acknowledged her dilemma, but there was no humour in his eyes.

Touching only the tips of his fingers, she rose. "Come, then, tell me all from Sir Hubert."

She moved quickly toward the arbour, obliging him to catch up with her, although he seemed to accomplish that easily enough in one leisurely stride.

"Sir Hubert?" she murmured. "Really?"

"Indirectly. On my way down from London, I happened to hear of a highwayman captured in Sussex whose identity was causing some problems for the local magistrate. From curiosity—"

"Of course," she murmured.

"From curiosity," he continued as though she had not spoken, "I took a short detour to the home of the magistrate, one Mr. Dunwoody, and was happy to identify the prisoner as the highwayman who robbed me and no doubt tried to hold you up too. There had been some doubt involving an army officer, apparently, but my testimony appeared to remove that and this Whitey is now bound over to the assizes."

"Did you get your horse back?" she asked lightly.

"No, the wretch must have sold him and spent my money."

"You seem to have come in to some more."

"The new rig?" He picked an imaginary thread off his sleeve. "Will it do?"

"Eminently."

He fished inside his coat and produced a folded document which he presented to her with a civil half-bow.

"What is this?" She frowned, breaking the seal and unfolding it to reveal a blank page. She lifted her gaze to his face and her heart turned over for here at last was the smile she had missed, shy and humorous and indescribably *necessary* to her sense of wellbeing.

"It's the message from Sir Hubert. I felt I should give you something to satisfy the curious."

She refolded it and stuffed it into her reticule. "You came here just to tell me this?"

"I thought you would like to know. I have more to tell you, too, though neither are really why I came." Before she could ask, he hurried on. "Smith's story turns out to be substantially true, apart from the one important fact of his name."

"Which is?"

"Lisle."

She blinked. "Lisle?"

"He is another nephew of the late Lord Sark, one Hunter, son of Carrington. Which makes him, I understand, the true earl."

"It does. Oh dear." She sank down on the arbour seat, inappropriate laughter tugging at her breath. "No wonder there has been a delay with Ralph's writ... He said it was because the poor king is mad."

"I'm rather afraid it is Ralph who has gone mad. Someone shot at Hunter-called-Smith outside the solicitor's office, and if it was not Ralph, I'm pretty sure it was someone sent by him."

Suddenly she didn't want to laugh anymore. "But Hunter has a son who also stands in Ralph's way... It is incredible, Jack, are you sure it is true? Could Smith have been lying to you?"

"He could," Jack allowed, sitting down beside her. "But I don't believe he was." He met her gaze and his lips curved ruefully. "You are right. I have little enough experience of people, but I have met all sorts over the last few weeks, and my judgments have always been substantially correct."

"No one is infallible."

"True. And I have alerted all authorities concerned, just in case."

"Is that why you stopped hiding?" she asked curiously. "To have the authority of the duke?"

"No." He hesitated. "I had already decided that. You were right at the Headless Horseman. Perhaps I needed my escape to find my way, and I did have a lot of fun. But it is time to do so openly. As myself."

"And so the world opens at your feet." She spoke lightly and yet her voice almost cracked, for she already missed her shy, mysterious young friend with the unique outlook and matching humour...

"And at yours, I see." Unexpectedly, he reached up and touched her hair.

Her breath caught until she saw the circlet of daisies hanging from his finger. She laughed, her face heating with embarrassment. "Oh, the devil, I forgot all about that! And here I was on my dignity among all the dowagers and dukes!"

"A token from an admirer?" he asked lightly.

"Oh no, only Durward. He is an old friend." She jumped to her feet. "Look, here comes tea. We should go back. Is there anything else?"

"Yes." He rose and again walked beside her, not touching. Was that his ducal dignity back in place? "Ralph is struggling for money, even with the earldom behind him. As part of Lily's settlements, I'm sure he plans to extract a personal payment from me that neither Lily nor the earldom could touch."

Tabitha frowned. "Can he really think you are so desperate?"

"I imagine the uncles must have painted me as such." He spoke with so little expression that she knew it hurt as well as annoyed. He cast her a quick smile, Jack once more. "They know I am here. I expect at least one of them within the next few days. I suspect you should also prepare for Ralph's arrival. Shooting at Hunter might well have been a moment of madness, but now he'll be determined to get Lily's imaginary dowry before news of the alternative earl is out."

Tabitha regarded him. "Do you know, before I met you, my life was dull?"

His smile dawned, sweet and yet heady in a way that was entirely adult. "Oh, so was mine."

She almost took his arm, but quite suddenly her eyes fell on Carily, throwing himself back on the blanket and attracting the attention of the three young ladies. "Watch your back around him," she said abrupt-ly.

"Who is he?"

"Lord Carily. He doesn't like not to be the centre of attention, and I'm afraid that will be you as long as you are here. Are you staying?"

He didn't answer, for they had returned to the chaperones' table, where he bowed her into the vacant chair. As if by magic, a servant placed another for him beside her. It was only as her tea was poured that she realized he had never returned her daisy chain. Either it sat forlorn on the arbour seat, or it was in his pocket.

Chapter Nine

The daisy chain crown was in his pocket, like a talisman. A silly thought, when it had been given to her by another man. A man he found himself rather liking—friendly, witty, carelessly at ease with all, unthreateningly flirtatious with the women but equally ready to join in intelligent conversation with them or anyone else. There was an appealing egalitarianism about him, and a recklessness that Jack secretly envied. Durward seemed to have laughed, danced, quarrelled, and duelled his way through life with equal fervour.

All Jack had ever done was bolt, run away from home like a foolish child. But he would waste no more of the life that had suddenly become as precious to him as it had always been to those who surrounded him. During tea, he watched and listened and strove to loosen his shy tongue just a little, carefully at first so that he didn't say anything stupid and then, gradually, with more confidence.

The attitudes towards him were mixed. There was a lot of awe, as though he were some mythical being suddenly sprung to life. Marriageable girls and their mamas were jostling for his attention. Everyone was curious, a few, like Lord Carily, ready to scorn and ridicule because he was no sporting Corinthian, but only so far for his rank conferred considerable protection. Jack found that faintly despicable. And he definitely did not like the possessive way Carily leaned over Tabitha.

She had warned him against Carily. Was that because it was Carily he had to win her from? Or was it Durward? This society was alien to him.

But he found, as he made his way inside with everyone else, that despite the novel jealousy, he did not care that she had taken lovers, provided he could win her love *now* and she would be true to him.

It had seemed such a fine idea in London. Here, among the attractive and sophisticated gentlemen who made up her world, he could not help feeling daunted.

"Your grace," murmured someone walking beside him, and he turned to see Lieutenant Meade.

"Someone else I need to apologize to," Jack said ruefully. "I beg your pardon."

"Oh, I can see the benefits of a *nomme de guerre*."

"Very good of you," Jack said, offering his hand, which Meade shook as though surprised.

"What did you learn about Smith?" he asked.

"I'll tell you in private. I seem to have been persuaded to join the party."

WHEN HE JOINED THE gathering in the gallery before dinner, there was already a jest floating around the company that he would be accompanied by a food-taster and his very own manservant to wash the ducal hands and wipe the ducal mouth. He pretended not to hear and was, in any case, welcomed with loud joviality by his host, Sir Peter Hawthorn, who gave him a glass of excellent sherry.

"I'm afraid your grace is the object of curiosity that must seem quite vulgar," Hawthorn confided with a hint of anxiety. "It's the novelty, you know, but it will die down."

"It's of no moment," Jack assured him. "I am only grateful for your kind hospitality with no notice and at a time when you must particularly wish me at Jericho."

"Good Lord, no," Sir Peter assured him. "You are quite the feather in my wife's cap—everyone will be talking about her party for months now." He flushed, adding endearingly, "Too honest?"

"There is no such thing," Jack said lightly. It was odd to find himself in the position of soothing his sophisticated host's social anxieties, but it gave him more confidence. People stared and joked because they didn't know what to make of him—which meant he was working from a fresh slate as he had wanted from the moment he had made the decision to leave Isley Place alone.

At last, he found Tabitha. She was with Lily at the centre of a lively group that included both Meade and Durward. Her beauty took his breath away, even as he registered that this was the part of her she showed the world. He had glimpsed the reality beneath, the inquisitive, vulnerable, warm young woman who had learned the necessity of a shell to survive an atrocious marriage. It was a lovely shell. But he wanted all of her with an intensity that made it difficult to concentrate on his host and the guests he was introducing.

Jack felt himself to be a somewhat fraudulent guest of honour as he was invited to escort his hostess to dinner. Any faint hopes he might have harboured about enjoying Tabitha's company on his other side were dashed immediately when he saw her being seated on the opposite side of the table by Lord Carily. On her other side was the young man who had been following Carily around during tea this afternoon.

On Jack's right, sat one of the chaperones he had met already, one Lady Kenwood, who might have been a formidable dining companion had he not had the benefit of many formal dinners with the aunts and uncles at Isley Place in celebration of Christmas, Easter and his birthdays. Entertaining Lady Kenwood proved to be unexpectedly familiar and easy to do —largely by listening, although she was eager to point out her youngest daughter, Amelia further down the table beside Lieutenant Meade.

On his left, he discovered his hostess was a great friend of Tabitha's, and suspected there must therefore be more to her than the ambitious and charming, if slightly silly, hostess. He took the trouble to draw her out, and found a warm, slightly chaotic young woman, devoted to her husband and young son, and to her closest friends.

"I owe so much to Tabbie—Lady Sark," she confided once.

"Oh?" he said encouragingly.

"Believe it or not," she said, her eyes dancing, "I was quite a handful as a young girl. Tabitha extracted me from my worst scrape and really made it possible for me to marry Peter —even though she suffered for it."

"Suffered?" he repeated, startled.

Lady Hawthorn hesitated, then leaned closer and lowered her voice. "You never met old Sark, did you? Vile old man. He cut her off from all her friends, read her letters and destroyed them when he chose. He happened to be away from home the day she—er... rescued me, and I stayed with her for several days. He was absolutely furious when he came home and found me there. She stood up for me, though, insisted I stayed until my mother came to collect me. Goodness, I am being indiscreet. Let me just say that if anyone deserves happiness, it is Tabitha."

She glanced along the table to where Carily was laughing at something Tabitha had said. There would be no happiness there. Jack knew it instinctively. But it didn't quite quell the jealousy.

Lady Hawthorn was obliged to give her attention to her other neighbour and Jack turned to the redoubtable Lady Kenwood.

When the ladies finally withdrew, many of them cast him curious and assessing looks on their way to the door. Tabitha did not. She sailed out with Lily's arm linked to hers, smiling as she listened to the girl's chatter. Lily glanced at him though, with more than a hint of apprehension. He supposed he should talk to her—or would that only frighten her more?

Without the ladies, the atmosphere was suddenly subdued. Jack felt like the spectre at the feast, inhibiting and unwelcome. Until Durward suddenly called down the table to him.

"I've just worked it out! The message you brought to Tabbie Sark—it was about the highwayman, wasn't it? *You* were the fellow he robbed!"

"I was," Jack said as everyone stopped talking to look at him, some with simple astonishment, others with gloating anticipation.

"Lose much?" Hawthorn asked.

"I was lucky to keep the coat on my back. The knave rode off with my purse, my pistol, *and* my damned horse."

Durward grinned. "Bad luck."

"Extremely," Carily drawled. "Your grace's entourage must have grown fat and lazy."

"On that particular day, I was quite alone."

"Not so much as a groom or a valet?" Carily said in blatant disbelief.

"Alas no."

"Your grace should have shot the scoundrel rather than hand over your pistol," said Carily's acolyte with a brave hint of contempt.

Jack raised his brows. "Do you think so?"

"Don't be an ass," Durward threw over his shoulder. "The scoundrel already had a weapon pointed at his grace. You'd have done the same."

"Wouldn't," muttered the boy.

Durward ignored him and again addressed Jack with genuine curiosity. "Were you more angry or alarmed?"

Jack considered. "I suppose I was a bit annoyed about the horse. But actually, it was quite exhilarating. I'd never been robbed before."

A few jaws dropped. Durward let out a shout of laughter. "That's the way to look at it!" He raised his glass to Jack, and added, "I shall cultivate that attitude. Because I know damned well I'd just fly into a rage at the injustice and get myself or someone else killed."

"Well, no one died at the time, though I don't fancy poor Whitey's chances at the assizes."

"And his capture was your message to Lady Sark," Durward said. He jerked his head toward Carily and his follower and possibly other devotees of Tabitha's. "*These* idiots were all getting jealous, imagining you were some unwitting go-between in a love affair."

"Why would she need a go-between?" Carily demanded aggressively. The implication being, presumably, that he was right here under the same roof.

"Exactly," said Durward with a hint of contempt. "You needn't try to sully the lady's reputation for your own gratification."

Carily glared at him, his face flushing with anger. "What the devil do you mean by that?"

"Nothing," Hawthorn said hastily. "He means nothing. And none of us will be giving Durward cause to flee the country again, will we?"

There were a few guffaws at that, particularly from the older gentlemen. Durward himself grinned good-naturedly and finished his port.

Hawthorn pushed the decanters around the table. "Drink up, gentlemen, and we'll rejoin the ladies."

"What is our entertainment this evening?" Barty Yeo, Tabitha's brother, asked.

"Your choice of cards or moonlight dancing on the terrace," Hawthorn replied. "If the rain stays off and if there is a moon!"

"Do you dance, Duke?" Carily asked, as though determined to find a tear to worry at.

"Up to a point," Jack said.

"What point?" Durward asked, apparently entertained.

"Gun point," suggested someone *sotto voce*.

"The point of foolhardiness," Jack said lightly, "on the part of the lady concerned."

"I expect you're a positive card sharp, then," Carily mocked.

"No," Jack said, bored. "This is excellent port, Hawthorn. Which merchant do you use?"

TABITHA HAD RARELY been so relieved to escape to the company of her own sex. She was annoyed with Louisa for placing her beside Carily again, for the man was growing increasingly impossible, as though he sensed something in Jack's arrival that was against him.

Unfortunately, it was inspiring him to show-off his closeness to her, as though she had granted him the right to touch her hand, lean too near, even stroke her leg beneath the table. He couldn't have known just how close to screaming that brought her. But she had every intention of avoiding him for the rest of the evening—for the rest of the week, in fact.

In the drawing room, she flopped onto a chair whose arms were too narrow for anyone else to perch on and thought with peculiar intensity of Jack. He had looked quietly stunning in dark evening dress, dignified without being haughty, handsome in a way that appeared tasteful and good-mannered rather than overly frail. All the same, she could see him unwittingly setting a fashion trend for that refined look and knew it would amuse him.

Not that she had watched him except from the corner of her eye occasionally, to be sure he was not struggling. He wasn't. He appeared to make Louisa laugh and even entertain the exacting Lady Kenwood without obvious effort. She wished he was beside her now, his company soothing, unthreatening, expecting nothing and yet...

He moved her. There was something about him that both aroused and melted her. He always made her think in different directions. And laugh. A mass of contradictions that inspired the same in her. He made her feel alive in a *good* way, and not a desperate, brittle sort of good either.

He would make someone the most perfect husband. How sad that it would not be her...

As though her thoughts had conjured him, he strolled into the room with Sir Peter, saying something over his shoulder to Durward that brought forth the latter's distinctive crack of laughter. Towards the back of the group, Carily entered, deep in conversation with Barty. That made her uneasy, too. But at least it kept him away from her.

"Is it dark enough yet for the moonlight dance?" Amelia Kenwood asked eagerly, causing a general ripple of excited laughter. Tabitha went out of the French windows with Louisa to gauge the weather. Footmen were summoned to light lanterns and torches and one of the dowagers, who had been a fine musician in her youth, took her place at the pianoforte, sorting through music. Tabitha supervised the placement of chairs and extra shawls, to make sure there were always two chaperones outside with the young people.

"How ridiculous that you and I should be chaperones," Louisa whispered with a gurgle of laughter. "I feel no older than these children!"

I do, Tabitha thought. *A lifetime older...* She ached for the growing up many of them would face. At least she would have some control over Lily's. Though when the first dancers spilled outside for the country dance set, she was not best pleased to discover Lily's first partner was Carily. He even threw Tabitha a look of triumph, as though he expected to have made her jealous.

The idea would have been laughable except she would not have him using Lily in such a way. The music began, drifting out of the drawing room windows quite clearly enough for the dancers. Although it was still only twilight, the sight of the graceful figures was both pretty and romantic.

Someone dropped into the chair beside hers, on the edge of the terrace.

"Wouldn't you rather be dancing?" asked the Duke of Isbourne.

"No. Wouldn't you?"

"Perhaps later. I wondered if I might ask Lily."

"You must ask whomever you like."

"I thought you would turn me down."

"I would when I am on chaperone duty. At least the young bucks appear to be sober."

"Hawthorn did swipe the port and brandy away rather sharply and marched us to the drawing room."

"A good effort, but they all know where it's kept. Is no one playing cards?"

"A few of the older fellows. Are you quite well, Tabitha?"

She blinked at him. "Of course I am. Are you? Or wishing you were back at Isley Place? Or carefree on the road?"

"Neither. I am perfectly content where I am."

The dance came to a graceful end amid much applause and happy laughter. Lily flitted over. "Oh, Tab, it's such fun to dance outside! You should try it! So should your grace," she added politely.

"I would love to." His grace had already risen. "Perhaps you would be my guide—I am not used to dancing."

Lily smiled at him and curtseyed before laying her hand happily on his arm. He bowed gravely to Tabitha and led his prize into the new set. Tabitha was feeling quite benign —until Carily slipped into the vacant chair.

It crossed her mind that he had engineered this, that he had sent Lily straight to her in the hope the duke would dance with her and leave the chair free. But perhaps she was being overly suspicious.

"Come for a walk with me," he said softly.

"I am on chaperone duty."

"Lily is perfectly safe with the Duke of Deathly Dull. Though she might need to bathe her poor feet afterward."

"Such a spiteful cat, aren't you, Carily? He dances as well as you." He did, too, and with no obvious guidance from Lily.

Carily watched them broodingly for a few minutes. "Aiming a bit high, aren't you? Considering the state of the Sark estate. Her dowry is barely respectable."

Tabitha sighed and pretended to smother a yawn.

"Oh, drat you, Tabbie, come for a walk," he exclaimed. He even took her hand as he jumped to his feet, aiming to pull her with him.

"I am about," she said between her teeth, "to make an utter fool of you."

He released her at once, though his expression turned ugly. "How long do you imagine you can keep me at arms' length?" he demanded.

"For ever. Go away, Carily, you've turned into a crashing bore." She waved him aside as though merely trying to see the dancers better.

He turned on his heel and stalked off into the drawing room.

JACK FOUND LILY'S ATTITUDE refreshing. She neither flirted nor gazed at him in awe as though he were some god come down to earth, which were the main responses of the other unmarried young ladies he had spoken to.

He had already taken a moment earlier in the evening to apologize for his less than honest introduction at the Headless Horseman, and now she seemed happy enough to carry on that discussion when the movements of the dance allowed.

"I don't in the least blame you," she said cheerfully. "It must be horrible to be constantly toadied and fawned over and cheated by innkeepers who imagine they can overcharge you."

"It has not happened to me much," he said cautiously. "In fact, I was merely playing truant and not ready to give up."

"What changed your mind? Tabitha?"

He smiled. "Yes. Is it so obvious?"

"Men do fall in love with her very easily," she said, a shade wistfully. "And who is she in love with?"

She gave him a rather adult look, as she spun away from him. When next they came together, she said, "You will have to ask her that. Is that why you asked me to dance?"

"Actually, no. I believe you are aware that your papa and mine have placed us in an awkward situation."

"Oh, that. Tabitha says we need not regard it."

"And what do *you* say?"

There was an annoyingly long gap as they danced with different people, before they again stood close enough to converse.

"You mean, do I want to be a duchess?" she said bluntly. "I'm sure it would have its advantages, and I do rather like you. But I have no intention of marrying anyone who is in love with someone else. Whether at eighteen or at eight-and-twenty."

He smiled, not even embarrassed by her insight, and for some reason her breath caught. "What a very sensible person you are."

"So are you," she said generously. "And you dance well."

They parted from each other in perfect harmony, and Jack, flooded with relief, looked about for Tabitha. Mrs. Saunders had replaced her in the chaperone's chair, so he strolled back into the house.

Chapter Ten

More than an hour later, Jack came across Mr. Bartholomew Yeo sitting alone on the terrace and looking rather white in the lantern light. The moonlight dance had ended, and the young ladies swept inside for tea. Jack, unused to quite so much company, had taken his tea outside for a moment's respite.

Tabitha's brother was about Jack's own age. Though clearly much more experienced in Polite Society, he seemed at that moment more like a struggling and anxious schoolboy. He didn't even notice Jack's emergence onto the terrace, until he sat in the other chair next to him.

Barty gave a start, followed by a rather mechanical smile. "Oh, it's your grace. Taking the air?"

"Just for a moment."

"Me too," Barty said and lapsed back into silence.

"Anything I can do?" Jack said casually.

Barty shook his head and clearly tried to pull himself together. "No. No, but I thank you. Just played a little too deep and lost. It happens." The careless smile might have worked on a face like Durward's, but on Barty it looked slightly sick.

"Isn't Lord Carily a friend who'd be willing to wait for his dues?" It was a guess, though a reasonable one. Barty had been playing cards with Carily for a large part of the evening, at first in a group, and then just the two of them. There had been a fixed look on Carily's face that Jack did not like and it had crossed his mind that Carily was punishing the brother for the sister's dismissal.

Barty's eyes flickered. "I'll come up with something," he said with a false brightness.

"Of course you will," Jack said. He gazed up at the sky. "I was fortunate enough to win on my brief flurry at the tables, so I'm in the happy position of being able to oblige a friend in temporary embarrassment."

There was a pause.

"Very good of your grace to put it like that," Barty said. "But in truth, you don't know me from Adam, and even if we were longstanding friends, I would not take advantage."

"Of course you wouldn't. But the offer stands. Strictly between ourselves." He lowered his gaze from the stars to find Barty regarding him with some curiosity.

"You're an odd sort of a duke, aren't you?"

"I don't know. I don't believe I have met any others."

Barty gave a snort of laughter and Jack smiled amiably back before rising and sauntering back into the drawing room with his teacup.

The company had thinned somewhat, with some guests having already retired and others preparing to do so. A few men and one of the dowagers were still playing whist. There was no sign of Carily. Or Tabitha.

When he had finished his tea, he bade the company goodnight.

"Past his bedtime," someone murmured.

Perhaps Jack imagined the difference in tone, more of a friendly ribbing now than contempt.

He went towards his bedchamber by a somewhat circuitous route that involved a tour of the lower floor before turning the wrong way at the top of the stairs. A watcher might have imagined he was lost. He wasn't. He was worried.

Not that he had any real reason to be. It was not even jealousy, for he had no claim on Tabitha and she certainly gave every impression of taking care of herself. But there had been something in Carily's manner that was both obsessive and spiteful. He hadn't necessarily cheated in his games with Tabitha's brother, but he had certainly gone out of his way to beat him.

The bedroom passages were all lit and he occasionally passed other guests. They wished each other polite good nights. But he had no idea where Tabitha's or Lily's chambers were, and he could hardly ask a servant without starting the kind of rumours he wanted to avoid. Nor could he wander the corridors all night on the off-chance she might need him.

And then, rounding a corner into what must have been the east wing of the house, he saw her.

She stood in a doorway, with light pouring out from the room beyond, and from the wall sconce behind her. She was very close to a man, her hands braced against his chest. Lord Carily held her with one arm around her waist, and one hand cupping her face.

For an instant, despite the light, Jack's world went dark. Hopelessness and jealousy seemed to halt his life, and yet he kept moving forward like an automaton because he didn't know what else to do. So many emotions battered him in that moment that he felt sick.

And then he saw the truth.

The pose that seemed so frozen in time for him, had in fact just occurred. She was straining away from Carily, her face blazing with anger. Her hands on his chest gave an almighty shove. He staggered back, apparently amused, drawing her with him, but she wrenched herself free and swung around.

She caught sight of Jack and stopped in her tracks. So did Carily, who had taken an urgent step after her. Her mouth was thin and set with fury, her turbulent eyes both appalled to see Jack and pleading with him.

And all this had happened in an instant of near silence.

Jack walked steadily forward until he stood beside Tabitha and halted. He could feel the trembling of her body in the air between them.

Carily smirked at him, clearly waiting for him to walk on, to pretend he had seen nothing. He even bowed in an insolent, half-hearted kind of a way that was somehow contemptuous of both Jack and Tabitha.

Jack did not return the bow.

"Good night, my lord," he said distinctly.

"Good night, your grace," Carily returned in some amusement.

Jack waited, giving her time to flee if she wished. That she didn't, hurt him unbearably. But it was Carily who was impatient, as though he couldn't understand why Jack lingered.

For her own sake, Jack willed her to go.

Carily seemed to finally understand that Jack was waiting for him to close his bedchamber door, for he let out a mocking little laugh.

Then Tabitha moved. She turned so that she was facing Carily once more. And took Jack's arm. Jack strolled on, as though it was just what he had expected. Behind them, Carily's door slammed.

"Take me outside," she said, low. "To where the air is clean."

THE WORDS SPILLED OUT as she thought them. Utter madness. He would escort her stiffly to her bedchamber door and leave her there with all the contempt she deserved.

He didn't. He kept walking until they reached the east staircase and turned down it with her.

She felt as though she were suffocating. She needed the cool, fresh air, though she could and should have gone alone. It was what she had intended. Only despite her shame in being discovered in such a position, by him of all people, his presence somehow soothed both her anger and her fears.

She had stayed with the Hawthorns several times. She knew the way out. She guided him to the side door, unlocked it and led him along the paths less visible from the house. Although the outside lanterns had been extinguished, there was enough light from the almost full moon to see their way easily.

"I have done you no favour," she said abruptly. "I have made you his enemy."

"I seem to have always been that," he mused. She gave his arm an irritated little shake and he glanced at her in surprise. "I'm not afraid of him."

"Perhaps you should be! Have you ever been in a fight in your life?"

"Oh, no. I am, sadly, protected by my rank."

"Sadly?" she repeated, startled.

"I find myself with an unprecedented itch to knock him down and hurt him."

Quite suddenly, all the tension seemed to leave her. She even sagged against him, holding tighter to his arm. "Then you do not believe I encouraged him?"

"I believe he assaulted you."

Even to herself, she had not called it that. Stupidly, her eyes prickled. "I had left Lily preparing for bed and was on my way to visit Louisa—Lady Hawthorn—I had something particular to say to her in private. Carily leapt out of his room as though he had been waiting for me and tried to embrace me. Apart from anything else, he startled me witless, so I boxed his ears. Unladylike behaviour, I know but he should not jump out at one."

"No," Jack said grimly. "He should not."

Her lips tightened again. "He seemed to think it was funny, and that he had only to kiss me to get me into his room, and I would submit as I really always wanted to."

"Did you?"

She frowned. "Did I what? Submit?"

"Always want to."

She rubbed her fingers hard across her forehead where a headache was threatening. "I thought about it," she said dully. "In Brighton. I found him attractive then, and I was so confoundedly bored. But something always prevented me—perhaps that he expected it. Or perhaps I was tired of the whole thing."

"What thing?"

She shrugged impatiently. "Being the wicked widow. Lovers. There was no love involved in any of my...flings, and I had finally recognized it. A little attraction, a little affection, but not love. It wasn't enough and never had been. I cared more about bringing Lily out respectably. He wasn't even supposed to be here, but he persuaded Louisa to invite him with the lie that he was madly in love with me."

"It isn't necessarily a lie, by his own standards," Jack said consideringly. "Though I would question his standards."

She curled her lip. "I have repelled him every way I know how. With gentle civility, citing my care of Lily, by the cold shoulder and blunt words. He doesn't seem to believe I mean any of it. Such a contemptible little act to make such a fuss over, but I won't do it, Jack."

He nodded as though he agreed, and it struck her that he did not quite understand. "I am not an innocent. I just need to choose. I have to be in control. No one will *make* me. Which is why I shall never marry again."

Even as she said the words, she knew no man could truly understand them. He would never know the horrors of being a wife, of the necessary submission to strength, to custom, to the law. To be fair, few women seemed to understand either. They were either lucky, or they just accepted.

She risked a glance at his face in the moonlight and saw the distinct crease of a frown.

"No true lover would ever *make* you," he said simply.

She rather thought her jaw was sagging, so she closed it. "Are you as innocent as you seem, my lord duke?"

"I might be naïve in some ways," he said tranquilly, "but I am not entirely innocent, no."

"You have been raking a swathe through the countryside since your escape?"

"No. Though there was a rather delightful tavern wench in Lewes. And the girl who looked after my rooms in Oxford. So I am not quite as pure as the driven snow."

A sudden warmth surged through her. "You are in any way that matters."

"So are you."

She peered up at him. "You really mean that."

"I do. You are simply Tabitha, and I love you."

He had a way of capturing one's breath. She could not even think, let alone speak, although emotion, tangled and wild, was flooding her.

He smiled, one of his sweet, apologetic smiles. "Forgive me. Such declarations cannot be what you want to hear right now. I shan't importune or seduce, but I wanted to be honest."

She stopped and so did he, turning his head to look down at her. All the muddle of contradictions seemed to resolve and fall away, leaving only an unlikely happiness.

Reaching up, she touched his cheek, felt the roughness of stubble and the smoothness above. "I would be very tempted," she said hoarsely, "to choose you."

Something exciting leapt in his eyes. He smiled in the way that dazzled. And she was only human. She stood on tiptoe and brushed his firm lips with hers. He held her gaze but did not move, and she realized he wouldn't, not because he didn't want to but because he had promised.

She liked that. She liked it very much. But her heart was beating hard in her breast and she *wanted, needed...*

"You may kiss me if you like," she whispered. *If you don't, I'll die...*

Very slowly, he lifted his hand in return and cupped her cheek. He bent his head in such a leisurely fashion that the anticipation made her gasp. He parted his lips, and she touched them with her fingertips, enjoying their texture, their faintest pressure as they moved inexorably nearer to hers, and finally closed on her mouth.

It was sweet. Tender. Did he still expect her to flee? Certainly he gave her several moments to draw back before he moved his lips against hers with infinite gentleness and slow-gathering sensuality. Her eyes closed. He tasted faintly of wine and coffee and Jack. His clean, masculine scent surrounded her, filled her, and his exquisite mouth sank deeper, adoring, pleasuring.

His tongue touched hers and with a sigh, she opened wider to him. Butterflies danced in her diving stomach. She pushed her arm up around his neck, stroking his nape, and his arms came around her, holding her against his slight yet hard body. No one had ever kissed her like this. It was heavenly.

She wished it would go on forever, but it seemed they both needed to breathe. He raised his head, and she opened her eyes.

"My," she said huskily. "Your tavern wench was a lucky girl."

He touched his finger to her lips. "Don't. This isn't about the past. This is now."

"I like now," she whispered.

"Oh, so do I." He kissed her again and she co-operated so fully, that he was breathing much faster by the time it ended. "I think, perhaps, I should take you back to Lily."

To her shame, her stepdaughter had fallen so far to the back of her mind that her name was like a jolt. She drew back and his arms fell away. She immediately felt cold, alone, until he drew her hand through his arm, and somehow it was still delightful to walk with him under the moonlight.

"Your grace is an excellent distraction," she drawled.

"My grace aims to please."

She thought it was probably true. Yet more than that, she knew she had moved him in return. There had been surprise as well as passion in his kiss. And that made her smile her way back to her chamber, to Lily, and to sleep.

LORD CARILY'S RAGE was all mixed up with frustrated desire and humiliation. And all in front of that puny whelp who, by rights or even common civility, should have the grace to be dead. And yet she walked off on the duke's arm as though he were some kind of prize!

What had that sickly puppy to offer a woman, compared with a charming, virile man like Carily? Nothing! And one could carry this game of "hard-to-get" too far, as he would show her tomorrow, along with his magnanimity. Meanwhile, there was nothing to fear from the little Duke of Death who would leave her at her door to dream of him, Carily.

All the same, he drank the remains of his brandy with some savagery and poured himself another large one, and then another.

He woke with some confusion, sprawled across his bed. A shaft of sunlight was blasting through the open shutter directly onto him, blinding him and making him sweat while the birds chirruped incessantly outside. His throat and mouth were parched, his head beating an annoying tattoo. It took several moments before he realized some of the knocking was on his bedchamber door.

His valet, damn the fool! Couldn't he just bring the damned tea without making such a fiendish racket? He snarled at the door, then sat up, clutching his head and ready to make the valet's morning as miserable as his own.

He peered at the figure who entered bearing a small tray. He was not valet-shaped. Carily peered closer.

"*Isbourne?*" he said in disbelief.

"The very same," said the Duke of Death affably. "I met your man at the door and persuaded to give up his tea tray so that we might have a chat." He deposited the tray on the bed beside Carily, looked about him, and placed a chair carefully before he sat in it and crossed his legs.

The little bastard was elegance personified, freshly shaved and clean, his morning dress perfection. Carily regarded him resentfully and poured himself tea with a hand that shook. He had really reached his alcohol limit before coming to bed. He shouldn't have had all that brandy in his room. He must have passed out, and now he felt dreadful. He didn't smell too pleasant either and he actually blushed at the sight he must present to this well turned out and cool young man.

"Too much brandy," he muttered and took a sizeable gulp of tea. It was no longer hot but he didn't care. "What can I do for your grace at this time of the morning?" It was meant to sound sophisticated and civil, but came out as merely bitter.

"Attend me, and believe me when I tell you I speak for Lady Sark. You are not to trouble her again by trying to speak to her, let alone by forcing yourself into her company. Should the opportunity arise, you will not invite her to dance or sit beside her. In short, you must stay away from her."

Total astonishment caused Carily's jaw to drop, reducing him to utter silence. For at least half a minute he could think of nothing to say to refute such insufferable arrogance. And then at last, it struck him and he began to laugh, to the imminent danger of his wildly sloshing tea.

"My dear fellow...! This ain't the marriage mart and you simply don't count with her. You cannot truly imagine you stand a chance with her, just because you are a duke?"

The duke didn't even uncross his legs. "No," he agreed. "But I am a gentleman, and so should you be."

"What did you say?"

"I am saying you must comply with Lady Sark's wishes. Your behaviour last night was most certainly not that of a gentleman. What did you mean to do? Knock her unconscious or compel her via the vowels you won from her brother?"

Carily jerked, as though he would jump to his feet and verbally blister the runt. But something very like shame seeped in with Isbourne's contemptuous words.

"Lady Sark deserves to be treated like the lady she is." The duke rose to his feet in one fluid, almost beautiful movement. "I do you the courtesy of believing you will now do so. If you don't, believe me, there will be consequences. She has many more friends than you do, and you are already here on sufferance. Good morning, my lord."

He strolled out of the room, leaving the door wide open. By the time Carily noticed, rose, and closed it, he was still utterly stunned.

Chapter Eleven

Tabitha was humming to herself while she sealed and directed letters for posting before breakfast. Her maid, Allison, was dressing Lily's hair.

"You're very happy this morning," Lily remarked.

"It must be the sunshine of your presence, my dear."

"Hmm."

There was a searching and rather pleased look in her stepdaughter's eyes that was new. "What are you concocting, Lily?"

"Me? Absolutely nothing. I danced with his grace last night."

"I know. I saw you. You looked very handsome together."

"He is a very interesting man, is he not? I believe I like him very much."

Tabitha paused, her fingers closed around the little pile of letters. "Do you?"

"Oh yes. He *is* handsome of course, and though Carily is right—he does look as if he would blow over in a puff of wind—he wouldn't, would he? And he has that kind of *inner* strength that so many louder men lack..."

"You guessed all this from one dance?" Tabitha managed. "Are you now considering obliging Cousin Ralph?"

"I don't believe the duke *would* oblige Cousin Ralph. In any negotiations, I would wager *my* money on his grace."

Tabitha straightened, regarding her stepdaughter almost blindly. He had said he loved her. He had opened her heart, and she would be the first to understand his attraction for a young and impressionable

121

girl. He would always do the right thing. Would that really include sacrificing everything to this marriage if he thought Lily wanted it?

Abruptly, she found herself hugged fiercely. "Don't look like that. It is not me he wants. But I'm so glad you like him."

Tabitha blinked, realizing with astonishment that the girl had tricked her into betrayal. "You...you *minx!*"

Lily laughed and danced away again. "Come, let's go down to breakfast—I'm starving."

Tabitha, leaving Allison smiling secretively over the hair brushes and pins on the dressing table, followed Lily from the room.

Sir Peter was presiding over the breakfast parlour, which was not busy. Only a few guests, dressed for a riding expedition, were eating there, discussing pathways and resting places. Carily was not among them, Tabitha was pleased to see. She did not want the happiness of her day spoiled.

Everyone wished the newcomers good morning, and Sir Peter went back to sorting through the pile of letters that had been brought up from the village.

"There's one here for Lady Lily," he said, when they had sat down near him with their chosen platefuls from the sideboard.

Tabitha passed the letter from him to Lily. She recognized the handwriting.

"Cousin Ralph," Lily said. She didn't quite wrinkle her nose, but from her unenthusiastic tone she might as well have.

Tabitha was only surprised it had taken him this long, though for the first time it struck her as delightfully funny. Ralph would be writing with some blatant excuse to bring Lily home—preferably without Tabitha—so that the girl would be at Sark Park to meet the duke. Who was in fact here. That really would make Ralph furious when Lily told him, though Tabitha hoped they might put off leaving a while longer.

Lily broke the seal and unfolded the epistle. Another paper fell onto the table.

"It's addressed to Lady Hawthorn," Lily said in surprise.

Tabitha passed it back to Sir Peter while Lily read the brief contents of her own letter with a wry smile. She handed it to Tabitha. "Portia is unwell and is asking for me," she said.

"I am very sorry to hear that," Sir Peter said sincerely. "And to lose you from the party. Can you wait until tomorrow? If you set off early enough you should be able to make the journey in one day. Will you go with her, Lady Sark?"

"That does not appear to be Ralph's plan," Tabitha said slowly, having read Ralph's stark commands. "In fact, he is coming here to fetch Lily."

"Oh, clever," Lily breathed. "Then you may more easily be left behind with perfect propriety. Only he doesn't know—"

"Well, we shall discover more when he arrives," Tabitha interrupted. "Though poor Louisa may find herself with another imposing guest. Perhaps he will put up at the village inn."

"We wouldn't hear of it," Sir Peter said hospitably. "Ah, good morning, your grace."

Tabitha looked up too quickly. Jack, once more in immaculate morning clothes, bowed to his host and to the room in general. Her heart was skittering like an impressionable schoolgirl's. The memory of his devastating kisses was so vivid in her mind that her body heated.

Fortunately, a distraction was provided by the riding party setting off with the rest of the company's good wishes, and in time, the duke came and sat on Sir Peter's other side. He had a modest plateful of smoked fish, egg, and a slice of toast. The servant poured him coffee and retreated to his post.

"What would you like to do today?" Sir Peter asked. "Louisa thought a restful day might be in order since we have the ball tomorrow, but of course you are not tied to the house. I'm not sure I have any more riding horses available today, but there are many pleasant walks, and a carriage ride to the seaside is not impossible if it takes your fancy."

"I don't know," Lily said doubtfully. "Should we wait around the house in case Ralph arrives?"

Jack's knife and fork stilled. He glanced up.

"His lordship is on his way to fetch Lily home," Tabitha exclaimed. "Apparently the countess is ill and asking for her."

Jack looked thoughtful.

"We don't even know if it will be today," Sir Peter said, "so I should do exactly as you wish." He rose and bowed. "If you will excuse me, I shall take my wife's letters to her. I'm sure she will be down shortly if you need anything."

"What a bore he is," Lily said. No one thought she meant Sir Peter.

"On the contrary," Tabitha drawled. "It will be most entertaining to see how he suddenly decides Portia's illness is of no consequence so that he might stay here and engineer your engagement to his grace."

Lily laughed, but Jack's attention was fixed elsewhere. He lifted the newspaper that Sir Peter had clearly cast aside in favour of the post.

"What?" Tabitha asked.

"Word is out," Jack said. "There is another claimant to the earldom of Sark." He lifted his gaze to Tabitha's. "A Mr. Hunter Lisle. From Canada."

TABITHA WAS ABLE TO cast off her unease about Ralph's arrival with surprisingly little difficulty. On Jack's invitation, they decided to take a walk around the countryside and enjoy luncheon at the village inn. Lieutenant Meade elected to join them, so in spite of everything, the day promised to be very pleasant.

Indeed, it was everything she could have hoped for and more. The weather was fine, with a light breeze to cool the warm sunshine, and the countryside very pretty. They strolled through wooded paths and along the bank of the nearby river, sometimes talking easily in a group, at others breaking into pairs. Although Lieutenant Meade's healing injury did not appear to trouble him, he provided the excuse for a slow pace and frequent halts.

It was all very relaxed and friendly, with, for Tabitha, the occasional thrill of Jack's hand grasping hers to help her over rough ground, or simply the sound of his voice, his very presence. The sense of humour that she had glimpsed before was more prominent today, subtle and yet joyful. He seemed wonderfully carefree, and to Tabitha, that was exhilarating.

Although they walked some distance, the duke showed no more signs of tiring than Nat Meade. She gathered that a month ago, he would not have risked it, but his weeks in the saddle had clearly strengthened both his body and his confidence. She began to suspect that for years now, his health had actually been better than his family had dared to hope. Smothering him in care had almost broken him rather than saved him. If he had not been so good natured, she thought, so reluctant to hurt, he would have thrown off all those yokes long since.

But he had found his way, without temper or acrimony, and she was proud of him.

Luncheon at the village inn was hearty and tasty, and the day seemed full of laughter when they eventually walked back to Hawthorn Court. With her hand in Jack's arm, Tabitha could not remember a happier day.

Until they came in sight of the house and Lily spoke with an air of resigned regret. "There is a carriage at the front. Ralph must be here to end our fun."

"Not at all," Tabitha said. "Merely a different kind of fun. It changes nothing, you know."

"Should we change before we greet him?" Lily asked mournfully. "He'll only scold about the mud on our skirts."

"Let him. I rather think he will have more on his mind."

The carriage had vanished, presumably around to the stables, by the time they reached the house. But Lily's plans to change her muddy walking garments were foiled when their host stuck his head out of the library. He was an easy-going kind of man and Tabitha was annoyed to see him looking positively harassed.

"Ah, there you are!" he said. "Do come in and greet our visitor."

"If he has been complaining about our absence to poor Sir Peter..." Tabitha muttered, metaphorically rolling up her sleeves.

"He won't for long," Lily said mischievously, swapping Nat Meade's arm for Jack's.

"You are a minx," Jack murmured.

"So Tabbie tells me."

Tabitha sailed first into the library. "I'm so sorry, Sir Peter, we—" She broke off, startled to be confronted not by Cousin Ralph, but by a complete stranger.

He looked her up and down expressionlessly and made the slightest, haughtiest bow.

Behind her, Jack said blankly, "Uncle Hazlett."

At that, the rest of the world ceased to exist for the visitor. Lord Hazlett strode forward, grasping Jack hard by the shoulders. "My dear boy!" He peered anxiously into his face. "Are you well? No! You are running a fever!"

Carily would have loved this, Tabitha reflected. Jack, clearly, did not, but just as she had imagined, he was patient with his uncle.

"No, sir, I have merely been walking in the sunshine. I am in perfect health and hope you are too?"

Hazlett blinked, as though the idea of anyone else's health mattering was preposterous. "I? Certainly, only anxious beyond—"

Jack cut him off, which Tabitha suspected was another first, although he spoke soothingly and with perfect civility. "There is absolutely no need for anxiety, sir, as I wrote to you. What a very pleasant surprise to see you here. But where are my manners? Allow me to make introductions. My lady, this is my uncle, Lord Hazlett."

Only good manners allowed his lordship to turn civilly to the rest of the company. He bowed again to Tabitha, this time with rather more respect, gathering she was a lady of rank.

"Uncle, this the Dowager Countess of Sark, her stepdaughter Lady Lily Lisle, and Lieutenant Meade, who is on leave from the Peninsular army."

Lord Hazlett, who had begun to look outraged as Tabitha was introduced, suddenly smoothed his brow and smiled with delight. "Lady Lily! I have heard a great deal about you. A pleasure to make your acquaintance. And you, sir, how do you do?"

"You must excuse us in all our mud," Jack said mildly. "We walked down to the river, Hawthorn—you have some lovely scenery here, and excellent land, too, by the look of it. Uncle, why don't you come up to my room and we can talk?"

As he ushered his eager uncle out of the door, he met Tabitha's gaze for the merest instant. His eyebrow twitched once, but it was enough to maintain the fragile connection between them.

Please don't let him fall back beneath Hazlett's thumb... All his life he had striven to cause his guardians least worry and unhappiness. It would be a difficult habit to break. Tabitha loved Jack's kindness, but was he really hard enough to move beyond that to the happiness of all? Particularly his own.

It was Lily who voiced the other main fear. "Something tells me Lord Hazlett is as set on this match as Cousin Ralph. We must prevent their alliance at all costs."

"What match?" Lieutenant Meade demanded, staring at her.

MEANWHILE, ANOTHER surprise awaited Jack in his bedchamber, where his old Oxford trunk stood open in the middle of the floor, and his old valet, Fox, shuffled toward him with tears in his eyes.

"Oh, thank God! Your grace lives!"

"Of course, my grace lives. I am perfectly hale and hearty. Very glad to see you, Fox, and the spare shirts and coats will be most useful." He patted the old man's shoulder, then left him to his pottering while he led his uncle to the two chairs positioned by the window.

"I'll own, Isbourne, I went into another blind panic when you wrote that you were coming here on your way home. The Hawthorns have a wild set about them, and you're not up to snuff, you know."

"Well, it is fun learning to be so."

"I hope you don't play cards for money?" Uncle Hazlett said anxiously. "And I'm sure you have not informed Lady Hawthorn's cook of your dietary requirements."

"Of course I haven't! I have already inflicted myself on her household uninvited, and to be frank, I have no dietary requirements."

Hazlett's eyes widened in horror. "But it has taken us your whole life to reach this stage! You must not—"

"Uncle, thanks to you and the others I have indeed attained good health. And I have never felt better. I am enjoying Lady Hawthorn's excellent meals." Though to be sure the Headless Horseman had not set a high standard, a thought he wisely kept to himself. "So tell me why you've come, Uncle?"

"To look after you, of course."

He smiled at his uncle but didn't release his gaze. "I do not require looking after."

Hazlett did not respond to that. Instead, he said, "At all events, I am pleased to see you on good terms with Lady Lily. She seems a perfectly charming girl."

"She is," Jack said coolly.

"You probably have not heard, but there has been some issue with the earldom, another claimant. The current Lord Sark—"

"Or not," Jack murmured.

"...assures me it is fraudulent nonsense. But even if it is not, it does not affect the girl who is indisputably the last earl's daughter. There are unfortunate connections, of course, but you may nip those in the bud after you are married."

Jack drew in his breath. "Uncle, you assume too much. Let me say at once that there will be no marriage between Lady Lily and myself."

Hazlett froze in the act of scratching his chin. "Eh? But...but why not?"

"Because she does not wish it. And frankly, neither do I."

Hazlett's astonishment was almost ludicrous, although he recovered quickly, drawing the full authority of his guardianship around him like a cloak. He had always been a stern if ultimately benevolent man, and his word had been law in Isley Place for Jack's entire life.

"Isbourne," he said impressively, fixing Jack with his most awe-inspiring stare. "You must and will do your duty."

"I fully intend to," Jack said quietly. "But my duty does not involve marrying that particular girl against her wishes because of some nonsense concocted by our fathers in their cups one night before we were born."

"It is *not* against her wishes!" Hazlett thundered in the way that had reduced Jack to trembling incoherence in childhood. "Sark has assured me she is willing, despite her silly stepmother filling her head with foolish notions. If she does not like you enough now, *court her.*"

Jack held his uncle's fierce, implacable gaze. He had not planned to have this conversation quite so soon. Putting it off until later was tempting in the present circumstances.

But that was what he had been doing for years, in case he hurt the feelings of his uncles, his nurse, his tutors, his doctors, his chaplain, his valet... It was why he had run away when he should simply have stood his ground. Only he hadn't been very sure then what his ground was. He had needed the space, the experience of being alone in the real world most people inhabited, to discover his capabilities and his goals and his true strength of feeling.

While Jack considered his best approach, the short silence seemed to unnerve his uncle, who shifted in his chair, fidgeting with his hands.

"I shan't court her, Uncle," Jack said. "I shall do my duty in my own way and in my own time, in the matter of my marriage as in all matters of the dukedom. I am grateful, as I have always been, for your advice and your views, but we are all aware that since I attained my majority, the role of the Trust has been merely advisory."

Colour flooded Hazlett's face, for this was Jack's tactful way of saying he had discovered from the solicitor what his uncles had hidden from him. In fact, they had misled him, but he refused to make the conversation one of grievances.

"The responsibility is mine, Uncle. I am ashamed to have used up so much of your life in my affairs, and eternally grateful for all you and my other uncles have done for me. But it is time I took up my own burden. Which means running my own estate, taking my seat in the Lords, and choosing my own bride."

He smiled and watched the agitation melt away from Hazlett's face, leaving it bewildered and oddly wistful.

"Shall we drink to your new freedom, sir?" Jack said, turning to find Fox tottering toward him. "A glass of brandy, if you please, Fox. There's a decanter on the mantelshelf."

"Very good, sir," Fox said. "By the way, since there is no dressing room for me here, I shall ask the housekeeper for a truckle bed to be made up in the corner..."

"You will not." Jack almost startled himself with the speed of his response. "Accommodation will be found for you with the other visiting servants."

The old man's jaw dropped, his eyes so hurt and accusing that Jack almost capitulated. Almost.

"Much more suitable," he added. "Um...the brandy, Fox?"

Chapter Twelve

Tabitha should have known that Cousin Ralph would turn up at a mealtime. He was the first person she saw when she and Lily approached the gathering in the gallery before dinner, standing out as he did as the only gentleman in morning dress rather than evening clothes. She could almost imagine his conversation with Louisa.

"Oh, no, dear lady, I could not impose. I shall put up at the inn just as soon as I speak to my cousin."

"We shall not hear of it, my lord. Do join us, and of course you must stay here."

"But I am not even dressed to dine!"

"Oh, that is of no matter. Truly, we insist..."

And so Ralph would have let himself be talked into what he had intended all along.

He stood now with Sir Peter and Mrs. Saunders, a glass of sherry in his hand.

"Rats," Lily muttered. "I thought we might have got away without him until tomorrow."

"He'll be trying to beat the rumour of his rival claimant. I wonder if he knows he is too late for that?" Several people had already asked Tabitha for the truth of the matter on her way downstairs. Since neither her own nor Lily's position could be altered by whoever succeeded to the earldom, it had been easy to maintain disdainful ignorance.

Accepting a glass of sherry from Chivers, Tabitha moved further along the gallery, searching for Jack. She would not let him be browbeaten by his family—although how she intended to prevent it was another matter.

"He has just come in," Lily said demurely. "With the terrifying uncle."

The girl was growing far too perceptive. Restraining the urge to stick her tongue out at her stepdaughter, she said, "You had best go and greet Ralph. I'll join you momentarily..."

As she hurried straight to the duke, she was relieved to see no obvious signs of distress in him. In fact, he looked handsome, elegant and confidant. And when he finally saw her, his whole face lit up and took her breath away all over again.

"My lady," he greeted her, as Chivers offered his tray. Lord Hazlett took a glass of sherry and one of lemonade which he handed to Jack. "Thank you," Jack said mildly, setting the glass back on the tray before Chivers could move away. "Sir Peter keeps a very fine sherry, at least as good as ours, Uncle—what do you think?"

"I think I see Lord Sark," Hazlett said coldly, taking his nephew's elbow. He had not acknowledged Tabitha's presence by more than the faintest inclination of the head.

"Don't let us keep you, sir," Jack said politely, and there was nothing for Hazlett to do, short of a physical manhandling, but to walk away.

"Is everything well?" Tabitha asked under her breath. "Are you?"

"Brushed through without tears on anyone's part, though old Fox was a bit of a facer. He's my valet who was my father's before me. When did Sark—or not-Sark—turn up?"

"Not long ago, I suspect. Have you heard the party gossip?"

"About Hunter's claim? I heard a few whispers. My uncle knows it, too. It must be all over London." He turned aside, walking a little further off from the crowd. "Tabitha, you must take care around Ralph. Don't be alone with him, or, in fact, go anywhere alone. He must be unstable to have taken a shot at Hunter like that—and you are in his way."

"Not when he knows you won't co-operate."

Jack's gaze flickered across the room. "Judging by the warm greeting between him and my uncle, neither has given up hope of persuading me. Oh, dear God." His breath of laughter contained as much frustration as amusement.

"What?" she asked following his gaze to where a dignified, balding stranger in a slightly threadbare evening coat was talking to Lady Kenwood. "Who is that man?"

"My chaplain."

She blinked. "You have a private chaplain?"

"Doesn't everyone?" Jack said flippantly. "In this case he must be Spiritual Authority to my uncle's Temporal."

"He's coming this way," Tabitha said. "Shall I leave you alone?"

"Don't you dare." He held out his hand to the approaching clergyman. "Dr. Wheatsheaf, what an unexpected pleasure. What brings you to Hawthorn Court?"

"Lord Hazlett, your uncle, requested my companionship." The man's handshake looked to have the grip of a wet fish. He peered closely at the duke. "Your grace looks exhausted."

"No, I don't," Jack said serenely. "My lady, allow me to present the Isbourne chaplain, Dr. Wheatsheaf. Sir, the Dowager Countess of Sark."

For some reason, the clergyman looked alarmed. "My lady." He bowed with considerable respect, though he cast a sort of imploring glance in the direction of Lord Hazlett, who was now with a group who included Ralph, Lily, her friend Amelia, and Lieutenant Meade.

"Ah, there you are, Tabbie," Louisa said, flitting past. "You must have known I'd partnered you with his grace. Lily is with young Meade. Come, Doctor and I shall introduce you to Mrs. Hart, who is a quite charming lady..."

"Bless her heart," Jack said.

"She is making up for Carily last night."

Jack leaned closer. "Plus, I did ask her."

"Did you?" Tabitha smiled and took his arm.

ANGER HAD BECOME RALPH Lisle's constant companion. Anger with old Sark, his uncle, for running the estate so poorly, for pretending to be so wealthy when he was not, for giving Tabitha effective control of Lily. Anger with the Lord Chancelor and all the other powers that be for never formally acknowledging the earldom was Ralph's, even though *everyone* knew he was his uncle's heir. Anger at the very existence of Hunter and his son, and positive fury that they dared cross the Atlantic to claim what he had always regarded as his own. He was also angry with both the sickly duke and Lord Hazlett because they hadn't immediately moved to fulfil their role in his plans; and with Tabitha for opposing his every move that could at least preserve something for Ralph and his family. *Tabitha*—a mere, silly young woman, and not even a Lisle by blood!

To all that constant rage, he now had to add anger at himself for not controlling it better. Although he had known in his heart that the man claiming to be Hunter Lisle truly was his cousin, the rightful earl, it had been somehow unbearable to see him strolling into *his* lawyer's office. It was a crazy impulse that had caused him to hide in the hackney waiting for Hunter; an even crazier one that had him lifting the pistol from where it had been so carelessly abandoned on the seat; and craziest of all to have aimed it and actually shot the man.

That had been stupidity born of the red fury blinding him. For even if he'd got away with killing Hunter, there was still a son before Ralph in the succession.

Now, the anger was still there, thrumming in the background as he laid plans for what he knew was his last throw of the dice. He meant to drag Lily home to meet and marry the Duke of Isbourne, even if it meant forbidding Tabitha the main house at Sark Park to do so.

"Oh, yes," he said to Lily now. "From insisting she was at death's door last night, Portia woke positively glowing with health this morning! I thought the best thing I could do was come in person anyway and calm your fears for her. My letter must have given you a terrible fright."

"Indeed," Lily said gravely, though he thought he saw a certain humorous gleam there that he put down to Tabitha's influence.

The lie was a weak one, but there was little else he could say when he discovered the duke was actually here. "So at least we are not obliged to disrupt your pleasure in Lady Hawthorn's party," he finished in a rush. "She tells me the Duke of Isbourne himself is among her guests—quite a coup! And have you met him?"

"Oh yes, and we like him very much."

Thank God. There would be no trouble from that quarter then. Even Tabitha might have withdrawn her objections. His luck had changed at last.

"Is he here now? Do point him out to me—discreetly, of course."

Lily, very pretty and demure in the palest pink muslin, looked about her and smiled. "There he is. Strolling toward us from the right. With Tabitha."

Ralph's fingers tightened on his sherry glass. A pulse beat rapidly in his temple. For he was sure he had seen that young man before. Pale and slight with contrasting black hair and refined, almost delicate features. Surely the same youth who had stopped to talk to Hunter Lisle outside the solicitor's office in London. When Ralph had fired that foolish shot. It was the duke himself who had hurried the man to safety, blocking any further shots with his own body.

For a moment, he was so overcome that his mind went horrifically blank.

And then he began to think again. Of *course* neither Hunter nor this man had seen him commit that folly. No one had. No hue and cry had gone up, despite the loudness of the shot, and Hunter himself was still very much alive, making lots of noise about being the true Earl of Sark. Damn him.

Ralph hoped his smile was not as sickly as it felt as Tabitha—*Tabitha, of all people!* —greeted him civilly and presented him to his grace.

Despite the pale skin and delicate appearance, the boy was not nearly as sickly as Ralph had expected. He had known in theory that he was two-and-twenty years old, but had pictured him as appearing younger, walking with a stick and a handkerchief held constantly to a pale, weak mouth.

There appeared to be little that was weak about this man. His eyes were intense and vital, and his movements were positively quick. Ralph pinned his hopes to the amiability of his expression, the friendliness of his hand-shake. If the duke was assessing him, he was, surely, giving him the benefit of the doubt at least.

Lady Hawthorn fluttered up to claim Ralph's escort into dinner, proving that he was still counted as the earl here. He held onto that thought as he realized the duke was escorting Tabitha with whom he seemed much struck.

While Lily walked into dinner beside a very junior army officer of no obvious account.

Oh, damn the woman! Must she make everything so ridiculously difficult? But he was learning. He squashed the anger and realized, gradually, that he could use Tabitha's encroachment— and the very useful if unexpected presence of Lord Hazlett and his chaplain. Ralph was, in fact, surrounded by allies, even if they didn't all know it...

He began his serious campaign immediately after dinner, when the ladies had withdrawn and the more relaxed, masculine atmosphere circulated with the port and brandy. After some general conversation and a bit of witty banter thrown between Hawthorn and Lord Durward from opposite ends of the table, a few more private discussions sprang up, and Ralph found it easy to move seats to settle next to Lord Hazlett.

"A pleasure to see you here, my lord. Quite fortuitous, in fact. How do you find his grace, your nephew?"

Hazlett shook his head in silent gloom.

"Really?" Ralph said. "I thought he looked surprisingly well."

"Oh, he *looks* well enough. But he has acquired an edge of stubbornness that was never there before. I'm afraid I have to tell you that he is now unwilling to budge on the matter of the marriage so close to your heart and mine. Which is a great pity, for now that I have met your cousin, Lady Lily, I am more convinced than ever that she would suit Isbourne to perfection."

"I believe you are right," Ralph said wisely, "especially since I had the pleasure of meeting his grace. But I believe I can discern the source of his grace's sudden opposition to the match. The dowager."

"I own I did not like to see him so much in her company but I cannot believe she would sabotage her stepdaughter's chances—"

"You must believe it, for it is the truth. Whether from mischief or malice or mere selfish interest, she has clearly tried to oust Lily and dig her own claws into his grace who, I gather, has not been about much in the world."

"Not at all," Hazlett said ruefully, "which I am beginning to think was a mistake on my part. I was trying to keep him safe, but it means he is not quite up to snuff."

"Certainly not against the wiles of a creature like the dowager. If she has not already seduced him, it is certainly her aim. Is he the sort of honourable man who would then feel obliged to marry her?"

Hazlett paled. "Oh yes. Most honourable. Most dutiful. I brought him up to be so."

Ralph smiled sympathetically, for he was grasping the depths of the fool's affection for his nephew, and saw that he would have to tread carefully, convince him of the terrible danger of not acting immediately. "One never expects such dutiful upbringing to work against one. Sadly... But I don't believe we have yet lost, my lord. You have an excellent and important young man, and I have a well-born and obedient young lady. And you and I together have all the wisdom they lack. I believe we must be bold and act quickly to save them from their own folly."

Hazlett shook his head. "I fear I have lost my influence over him. Just a few short weeks and—"

"Nonsense," Ralph said briskly. "That will be Tabitha's doing. She is rebellious and chaotic by nature. Also, insatiable and erratic. She will move onto her next conquest, whether or not she secures the dukedom first. I doubt he is of the necessary strict nature to keep her in line and so all your efforts to secure the dukedom will be for nought when you find—forgive me—a cuckoo in the nest. To say nothing of poor Isbourne's personal misery."

Hazlett's eyes widened. "She is really as bad as that? One hears rumours, of course, but—"

"With cause," Ralph interrupted brutally. "The late earl, my uncle, had a terrible time disciplining her. Since his death, no one can control her. I try to conceal what I can, of course, for she shames our whole family with her antics, but to you, sir, I must be honest. I can see at least two of her paramours without turning my head. Durward there, wild to a fault and still expecting his man to die from his last duel. And Carily, a positive rake who scandalized Brighton by his relationship with her only a couple of weeks ago. She is the harpy—I'm sorry, but I use the word advisedly—who threatens your unworldly nephew."

Hazlett was suitably appalled, his lips a mere line in his white face, his bulging eyes hardening in the most gratifying way.

Ralph struck while the iron was hot. "We must act at once. I told you I would procure a special license, and I have. You have brought the chaplain."

Hazlett drew a breath. "Yet our principal players are unwilling, which brings it all to naught."

"Convince your chaplain," Ralph said simply. "Believe me, there are ways to convince the bridegroom and in such straits as this, I am willing to use all of those ways. Our best opportunity will be during tomorrow evening when the ball will occupy everyone in one place."

Hazlett reared back. "We cannot abuse the hospitality of our hosts!"

"Of course not," Ralph replied, thinking fast. "We should obviously invite them and swear them to secrecy until the happy event is complete and they may announce it to the world. I have brought all the documents as we agreed. Believe me, Hazlett, we will save our beloved young people in spite of themselves."

TABITHA HAD NO SOONER accepted her morning coffee from Allison, than Louisa whisked herself into the room, fully dressed, and sat on the edge of the bed for a gossip.

"So," she said cozily. "You and the duke."

To her annoyance, Tabitha felt herself blushing like a debutante with her first admirer. She lifted the cup to her mouth giving herself time. Apart from the arrival of Cousin Ralph and the disapproving Hazlett, yesterday had been rather wonderful and she wanted to hug it to herself, not contaminate it with the opinions of others, even her friends.

Louisa said encouragingly, "I like him. There is something very charming about him. And as for his smile... I would almost leave Peter for that smile."

Tabitha smiled. "No, you wouldn't."

"No. But he certainly isn't the jest everyone expected him to be, is he? He might not fit the mould of the fashionable Corinthian, but that mixture of shyness and wit is really rather devastating, especially with those looks. And he is not remotely haughty once one knows him."

"No," Tabitha agreed. Although there was nothing shy about his kisses. There had been another of those last night at parting—secret, silent and utterly seductive. On top of the day spent in his company, learning so much more about him, it had led her to a terrifying conclusion.

She had caught glimpses of his appallingly joyless, lonely past, his current, wide-ranging thoughts, his almost miraculous sense of humour, his basic, decent kindness... And she was lost. She loved him.

What the devil was she to do about that?

"Will you marry him?" Louisa asked.

The cup seemed to jerk in Tabitha's hold and coffee sloshed into the saucer. "Of course not," she said crossly. "I am not cut out for marriage."

"You are not cut out for marriage with a particularly nasty old man. Who is?"

"I have learned my lesson and will remain happily widowed. His grace deserves a lovely, unsullied young girl."

"Like Lily?" Louisa said provocatively.

Tabitha scowled. "No. Lily is not ready for marriage."

"Don't break his heart, my dear," Louisa said, rising to her feet. "I had better be off—much to do today with the ball this evening!"

She bustled away, leaving Tabitha staring into her coffee.

"Don't break his heart." She could already feel the shattering of her own. And yet she had barely known him a fortnight.

What do I do? How do I make it right?

God help her, she didn't even know what *was* right anymore.

Making him happy. If anyone deserved happiness, fun, joy in his life, surely it was Jack.

Could those things possibly be with her?

Or should she walk away before she caused any more pain? She had the lowering feeling it had to be one or the other.

All or nothing.

Chapter Thirteen

Although Tabitha secretly longed to spend every waking moment with Jack, she forced herself to avoid him. In this, she was abetted by Louisa's clear need of a lieutenant to run errands and generally help with last minute preparations for the evening's ball.

She took time away from this hectic activity only to be sure Lily was safe under the temporary chaperonage of Amelia's mama, who was seated in the garden beneath a chestnut tree while a group of young people sat around her, alternately reading, chattering excitedly about the evening's ball, and playing pall-mall.

Tabitha had glimpses of the duke, when she cast him a distracted smile, but never paused to speak to him. Even at luncheon and tea, she sat close to Lily and tried not to look at him. He seemed to spend much of the time listening patiently to his uncle, and to the chaplain she gathered had never been a favourite with him. No doubt they were still trying to persuade him into marriage with Lily. Oddly enough, his relief from this dull work was with Lord Durward, who made him laugh. An unlikely friendship appeared to be forming there. Aching, Tabitha thought it would be good for both of them.

"Has Ralph been pestering you?" Tabitha asked Lily quietly as they walked back toward the house.

"Oddly enough, no—or not beyond remarking once how well his grace had turned out and how lucky his duchess would be. Which is true, you know."

There was a soft gleam in the girl's eyes that Tabitha had never seen before. It caused a stab of fierce pain.

Is that how it is to be, after all?

It must be for the best.

If, if, it leads to her happiness and his...

Dinner was early, as tea had been, a formal but light affair to which several of the Hawthorns' favoured neighbours had also been invited, some from quite some distance away. More yet would come to the ball.

But the biggest surprise at dinner, was the guest accompanying the local vicar.

Tabitha and Lily had just arrive at the pre-prandial gathering in the gallery, when they were joined by the duke.

"I suspect either my uncle or your cousin has been importuning Lady Hawthorn," he murmured to Lily. "For I am to escort you to dinner."

"Oh, bad luck, your grace," Lily laughed.

Tabitha smiled a little blindly as he transferred his gaze to her. "I believe you are with Lord Durward."

"Then at least I shall be entertained," she said.

As Lily turned to greet Amelia, he leaned closer. "Is something wrong?"

"Of course not," she said brightly. "Apart from the presence of Ralph and..."

"Indeed," he interrupted softly. His gaze had flitted beyond hers and she turned her head to see the approaching group of people, one of whom seemed to be vaguely familiar though she could not quite place him at first, out of context as he was.

Then Chivers made his announcement, and she realized he was the vicar's guest. "Mr. and Mrs. Teague, and Lord Sark."

Hunter Lisle stood between the vicar and his wife and bowed in the sudden silence. The Hawthorns hastily welcomed their guests. Louisa's colour was considerably heightened, and Tabitha gathered their hosts were as shocked as the other guests.

Someone let out a rather delighted giggle. Through the hum of excited conversation starting up, Tabitha distinctly heard Ralph's voice blustering, "Outrageous! Utterly unacceptable!"

"It is certainly blatant," Jack murmured. "Now they are both using the title neither is quite entitled to as yet..."

"Oh dear," Lily said torn between nervousness and laughter. "Cousin Ralph will be incandescent..."

He was. White faced and tight-lipped with fury, he could only watch from the corner as everyone surged toward the new claimant. It was rampant curiosity, of course, the scent of scandal and gossip in their nostrils, but to Ralph it must have looked like support for his enemy.

"I am almost sorry for him," Tabitha murmured.

"So would I be if I wasn't so sure he had tried to kill Hunter already..."

Hunter was graciously accepting introductions and shaking hands, but through a sudden space in the crowd around him, he suddenly saw Jack. His whole expression changed from calm civility to sparkling pleasure. He advanced through the crowd that parted for him, his hand outstretched. "Your grace, my dear fellow! What a delightful surprise!"

Tabitha took Lily by the elbow and drew her back a step—she did not want Lily associated with either side of the quarrel.

Hunter, however, had concentrated all his attention on Jack, shaking his hand with genuine warmth.

"This man saved my life—literally!" he declaimed to his hosts and the vicar and anyone else within earshot. "If it had not been for his hurrying me away, actually placing himself between me and a bullet, I should have been shot through the heart."

"That's not quite how it happened," Jack protested.

Hunter waved that away. "If I had not recognized you, I wouldn't have moved to shake your hand."

"Then it was your own action, sir, not mine, that saved you."

Of course, Jack's disclaimer only led people to think all the more of him for his modesty, and he actually flushed under all the admiring gazes, looking more uncomfortable than Tabitha had ever seen him.

Hunter grinned and clapped him on the back in a friendly way, while he repeated the story of his attempted "assassination" to all and sundry.

"I suppose they have not found the shooter?" Jack asked.

"Not yet. I took the advice of the authorities in London and decided to come down to the country to look up my old friend Teague, whom I knew in Canada when he was engaged upon missionary work there..."

"Well," Lord Durward murmured in Tabitha's ear, "this should prove a more interesting evening than anyone imagined! A man of parts, our modest little duke."

"I don't find him little," Tabitha said defensively. It should have pleased her, not hurt her.

"Neither do I," Durward said. "Rejoice, Tabbie, I'm to partner you to dinner."

As Jack turned to find them again, Tabitha took Durward's arm, leaving Lily to the duke. Oddly, she caught Lord Hazlett's disapproving eye, and she was sure his lip curled.

DINNER FELT LIKE SOMETHING of an ordeal. Although Durward was much his usual, entertaining self and, on Tabitha's other side, Mr. Saunders, the father of Lily's friend, was an amiable gentleman with twinkling eyes, she felt ridiculously tense, almost brittle. She knew she talked too much and laughed just a little too loudly, as though she was trying to rush through the whole event.

And the ball was still to come.

Tabitha loved to dance, so she had been looking forward to the occasion since leaving Brighton, all the more since Jack had joined the party. Now she had a headache behind her eyes and wanted only to be somewhere else.

Had Lily not been present, she would probably have made her excuses and taken to bed. But she could not spoil her stepdaughter's first formal ball. Nor admit that she was not a suitable and dutiful chaperone.

And so, after dinner, she helped dress Lily for the ball and was so pleased with the result of her appearance—an angelic beauty in white muslin and net trimmed with rosebuds—that she almost stopped worrying. Quite what her anxiety was—apart from foolish jealousy and indecision over Jack—she did not know. The evening just felt suddenly... ominous.

She hoped Ralph was not about to take another pot shot at Hunter.

The duke, as the highest-ranking guest, opened the ball by dancing with Louisa. And since Lily had promised the first dance to Lieutenant Meade, Tabitha, as the lady of highest rank, was happy to dance with Sir Peter.

They were comfortable enough in each other's presence for him to mutter, "Such a nightmare! What the devil are we supposed to do about the two Lord Sarks?"

"Avoid introducing either of them to anyone," Tabitha advised. Ralph, talking to Lord Hazlett, found the time to glare at her in disapproval. Hunter seemed to be making more friends, the centre of a laughing group. "Fortunately for Louisa, neither are at an age where she should feel obliged to find them dancing partners! But I am sorry, sir. I wouldn't have had this happen for the world."

"Then you didn't know he was coming here?"

"Lord, no, and neither did his grace. When we ran into him—at an inn when I was on my way here—he did not call himself Lisle let alone Sark. He had just entered the country, I believe." They parted in the dance, met again, and turned together. "Don't look so worried. Louisa's party will be talked about for years, whoever turns out to be the true Sark!"

With perfect propriety, Nat Meade returned Lily to her side after the first dance, although she was almost immediately snatched up again by another young man. Tabitha took her place among the dowagers and chaperones, although a court did develop around her. She still managed to keep her eye on Lily, however, and this time the girl didn't come immediately back to her side. Instead, she let her partner give her a glass of lemonade and strolled with him until the next dance started up, and Barty claimed her.

Tabitha relaxed and rejoined her court, which did not, she was glad to notice, include Carily, who hadn't bothered her at all since the night he had almost dragged her into his bedchamber. A few asked her to dance, but she insisted she was merely chaperoning. The duke, who had wandered over during the third dance, overheard her and did not ask. Keeping determinedly to her own rules, she offered him no encouragement, no opportunity for a private word.

Barty brought Lily back to her side, where the girl happily consumed the rest of her lemonade, her eyes sparkling, her manner animated and happy. Tabitha ached for her innocence and wished it could last forever.

"May I ask Miss Lily to dance?" Durward asked Tabitha, so she knew he would behave.

As they went off, Barty slid into Lily's vacant seat. Glancing at him, it came to her that he looked happier than he had for a couple of days.

"You're looking rather pleased with yourself," she said lightly.

He grinned. "Actually, I am. I enjoy a good caper. Besides, I've just had a talk with Carily."

"Oh."

"He's not such a bad fellow, you know. He beat me soundly at cards the other night and I'm afraid I ended up owing him rather more than I can comfortably pay. I went to pay what I could and grovel for permission to pay the rest next quarter day. And do you know what he did? He tore up my other vowel and said I'd written out a duplicate by mistake and my debt was paid. I argued, of course, but he was adamant. Unexpectedly handsome of him, don't you think?"

"Yes," Tabitha said slowly, for Carily never did anything without a reason. Angry with her, he had clearly fleeced her little brother. Why would he forego that money? He had given few hints of a conscience until now.

Barty lowered his voice. "He also said he'd had a talk with the duke and decided he wasn't a bad fellow after all. Made him think, he said. And said the duke deserved you where he didn't. I thought that was pretty handsome, too."

Perhaps it was. Perhaps all he had ever needed was a jolt. Mostly, she wondered what on earth Jack had said to him. It had certainly worked wonders.

As the dance came to a close, Lily stopped to talk to someone—Lord Hazlett, Tabitha saw with some surprise. Surreptitiously, she looked around for Ralph, and to her annoyance saw him stalking toward her.

She turned aside to accept a glass of champagne from one of her admirers, and hoped Ralph would take the hint. He didn't, merely stood beside her until she was forced to notice him.

"Cousin," she said civilly. "It is an excellent party, is it not?"

"Clearly," he snapped. "A word in private if you please."

Unhurriedly, she set her glass on the table and rose to her feet. "Let us walk, then." She lowered her voice. "But if you make a scene, Ralph, I shall walk away."

"Please don't adopt that self-righteous tone with me. You are supposed to be chaperoning Lily, and she is running wild, dancing with rakehells and nobodies while you flirt with all and sundry. It won't do, Tabitha. It won't do at all."

"It wouldn't if it were remotely true. She has danced only with young men who are known to me and who asked me for permission first. Lily is a sensible and well-behaved girl who would never leave my sight let alone give me cause—"

"*Then where is she?*" Ralph interrupted with sudden intensity.

Tabitha glanced to where she had last seen her stepdaughter. "She was speaking to Lord Hazlett..." But she was not there now, nor could Tabitha see her in the throngs circulating before the next dance.

Ridiculous panic surged, no doubt fed by the seriousness of Ralph's tone. The truth, of course, might lie in the fact that neither was there any sign of Nathaniel Meade.

"I'll look for her on the terrace," she said abruptly. "She probably needs cool air after all that dancing. In case she isn't there, you should inquire—discreetly—of Lord Hazlett, which direction she took."

Without a further glance at him, she strolled casually to the French windows and out onto the terrace. She was so sure that she would find Lily there with Meade and have to haul the pair of them back into the respectability of the ballroom, that when she found the terrace completely empty, she felt curiously forlorn.

Surely they would not have been foolish enough to go alone into the gardens? The terrace was lit up, but the gardens were not, being rather too secluded for this kind of event. As Tabitha well knew, having walked and kissed with Jack there...

Quickly, she ran down the steps from the terrace and across the wet grass. Lily would owe her a new pair of dancing slippers after this...

Something bumped, like a loose door, away to the left where there was a little summer house and a gardener's shed. Surely Meade would not have taken her there!

And yet, as she knew from experience, a summer house was an excellent place for an assignation. She turned in that direction, peering into the darkness. A pale light shone, and she quickened her steps.

She reached the summer house door, which was closed. But the light flickered to the left and further back. Something—some-one—moved. She was sure she heard breathing. Were they avoiding her by hiding in the gardener's shed?

This is ridiculous! She marched toward it and found the door wide open.

"Lily," she whispered.

And something struck her hard between her shoulder blades. She staggered forward into the shed and it slammed shut behind her. The bolt shot home and footsteps receded, not toward the house, but in the direction of the stables. And there was only one set. No one spoke.

The darkness of the shed was absolute. So was its silence. She was alone. Stunned, her heart hammering with fright, it took her a moment to be clear what had happened.

Ralph. Ralph had done this, using one of his thuggish grooms who probably didn't even know it was the dowager countess he had been or-dered to lock in the shed. Why?

Whatever the reason, it could not be good. She needed to get out and prevent whatever it was. What on earth could she prevent? She had no say in the adjudication between himself and Hunter as earl, and no evidence that would help either of them.

But she *could* prevent Lily's marriage.

Hazlett. The chaplain. If Ralph had a special license…

Jack will not do it. He will not marry Lily, and certainly not like this! In the middle of someone else's ball.

Then Ralph will make him. Somehow, he will find a way to force him, hurt him. She had to get out of here! In desperation, she tried pushing and kicking at the door, but both it and the bolt were solid, and she wore the flimsiest of shoes. She was more likely to break her own toes.

If she shouted, would anyone hear? And if they did, what kind of a scandal would that cause, to be discovered out here alone in the dark?

Ralph would at last have the ammunition to challenge her guardian-ship of Lily. No, she must get out on her own.

She moved around the shed and by means of touch raked through the various garden tools, pots, and bottles, looking for something, any-thing that might help to weaken the bolt. She could try hitting the door with a mallet...

A saw! Unfortunately she found it by cutting her finger on it, but she lifted it with considerable triumph and felt her way back to the door. It slid easily into the crack at the side of the door, and she brought it downward until it struck the steel bolt.

She drew it back and began to saw.

It was hard work, and she had the feeling she was not getting very far. Panting, she paused for breath.

A voice beyond the door said warily, "Lily?"

JACK WAS WORRIED.

Despite the gaiety of the ball and the success of his efforts so far to negotiate the social maze of strangers, flatterers, fun-pokers, im-portuners, and matchmakers, something was wrong. The presence of Hunter Lisle and his embarrassing efforts to paint Jack as a hero made him uncomfortable, particularly when they were believed. He also did not like the intimacy he noticed between Uncle Hazlett and Ralph. And he particularly did not like the change in Tabitha.

He had looked forward to more of her company, to dancing with her, perhaps stealing a more intimate moment on the terrace. But she seemed to be avoiding him, concentrating on her duties to Lily, as was only right, while still managing to hold court in a manner that some-how froze him out.

He could have coped with that—a man as sheltered as he could surely not hope to hold the interest of a woman like Tabitha for very long—but her aloofness was too tense, somehow. Worse, the glow of happiness had faded from her eyes, from her smile, from her very person. And he could find no reason for it.

He looked around for her friend Lady Hawthorn, who, as hostess, no doubt had enough on her mind, flitting hither and thither in her bright jewels and beautiful gown like a butterfly in a wildly blooming garden. Lily, however, might have some clue as to what was upsetting her. Except he could not see her on the dance floor, or...

"Your grace."

Jack turned his head to find Lord Carily, of all people, standing in front of him. "My lord."

Carily gave a faint, uncertain smile. There was a new diffidence, almost humility in his manner.

"I have been thinking a great deal," he said seriously, "about our recent conversation."

Jack inclined his head.

Carily glanced about him. "Might I ask—beg—five minutes of your time in private? Your grace has made something of an impression and I think I need...that is, I would like...a little more clarity. Someone to clear my head with, if you see what I mean."

Jack, used to figuring things out for himself, did not, quite. But Carily had known Tabitha considerably longer and might well provide insight into her sudden change.

"Of course," he said politely.

"It is somewhat crowded here for a private conversation... Perhaps the library...?"

Again, Jack inclined his head, and they walked together around the edges of the ballroom to the door. He could not even see Tabitha now.

The public rooms were in darkness, since all the facilities necessary for the party were catered for in the ballroom annexe. However, the library appeared to be an exception. Although the door was closed, a band of light shone beneath it. Carily opened the door and bowed him inside.

Jack walked in and pulled up in surprise. The room was far from private.

Uncle Hazlett was there, with Dr. Wheatsheaf. So was Lily and, most worrying of all, Ralph Lisle. They were all standing and looking awkward, apart from Lily, who had drawn herself up to her full height and was glaring at her cousin. When Jack walked in, she transferred the glare to him.

"How could you?" she said brokenly. "How could you treat Tabbie so?"

Jack blinked in astonishment. Behind him, someone else came in—the Hawthorns, wreathed in smiles.

"What a unique and romantic way to celebrate a wedding," Lady Hawthorn exclaimed. "And no wonder Tabitha was so reticent about your grace! I had it all wrong in my head."

Carily closed the door, turned the key, and pocketed it.

Jack turned slowly and faced his uncle. "What is going on?" he asked evenly. "What wedding?"

Uncle Hazlett smiled a little sadly. "Yours, my boy."

"Tell him it is nonsense, your grace!" Lily said furiously.

"Arrant nonsense," Jack said, taking in the bewildered faces of his host and hostess. He turned to Lily, offering his arm. "Perhaps I might escort you back to the ballroom and Lady Sark."

"Lady Sark is not there," Ralph said at once. "She is...indisposed."

Jack took a step nearer him, his arm dropping back to his side. "Where is she?"

"She will come to no harm. Providing you do as we require. Sign the papers and marry my pretty cousin. Where is the hardship in that?"

Jack's blood ran cold. A muscle jerked in his throat. "What have you done to her?"

"Wait a minute," Sir Peter said, frowning suddenly. "I don't like the sound of this at all! Are you trying to *compel* Lily to marry his grace?"

"I positively insist upon it," Ralph said, almost casually. He was examining the nails of his right hand. "She is not safe with That Woman. His grace is not safe with That Woman! The only solution, as Lord Hazlett and I see it, is for Lily and his grace to marry each other immediately for their own safety, negating That Woman's foul machinations."

Sir Peter and Lady Hawthorn both opened their mouths to object, but Jack was before them, contempt dripping from his every pore.

"If you are referring to Lady Sark, you are a viler creature than even I imagined. And *you*—" He swung on his uncle, catching and holding his gaze. "I could never have imagined you would stoop so low. As for you..." He looked Dr. Wheatsheaf up and down. "Where are the strict Christian principles you have always preached to me? How many clear commandments have you broken this evening?"

Neither his uncle not Wheatsheaf would meet his gaze.

Hazlett said hoarsely, "It is for the best, Isbourne. You must be safe."

"*I?*" Jack said, rare rage suddenly swelling up from his toes to consume him. "I alone, of all the people in the world, must be safe? Lady Sark does not count? Lady Lily does not count? Your kind hosts do not count that you break all the laws of hospitality to deceive them? Oh, no, this stops here! And if you have harmed one hair of Lady Sark's head, I will prosecute the lot of you with the full force of the law!"

His sudden anger, which he doubted even his uncle had seen before, seemed to overawe them all. He had even swung on Carily, his hand held out, palm upward for the key, when Ralph spoke again—unworried, faintly amused.

"And if Lady Sark survives your betrayal of her, how will her reputation survive such prosecution? Especially after her long disappearance tonight. How will Lady Lily's?"

Jack spun to face him, and Ralph actually backed away.

"You wouldn't," Lady Hawthorn whispered, staring at Ralph in horror.

"I would," Ralph said self-righteously. "I would do anything to save my cousin."

Dear God, he was almost convincing. And Jack did not doubt he would do his worst. But the immediate, physical fear for Tabitha overrode everything. He had to get to her now, find her, wherever she was.

He strode across the room and hurled himself at Carily, slamming him into the door. "The key, you commoner! Right now. Or I swear to God, I'll batter my way through with your head."

Surprised and winded as he was, Carily let out a shout of laughter—which suddenly choked off as Jack closed his hands around the man's throat.

Carily jerked and scrabbled at the relentless hands. But Ralph threw himself forward, gripping Jack's arm, hauling him off, and allowing Carily to fight back.

Jack had no intention of making it easy, and he didn't. Only once did he glimpse his uncle's face, which bore an expression of undisguised horror.

Chapter Fourteen

"**L**ily?"

The whisper was unrecognisable to Tabitha. Had someone mistaken her for Lily when they had pushed and locked her in here? Was this a friend or an enemy?

"No," she said clearly. "It's Tabitha."

"Lady Sark!"

Unmistakably, that was Nathaniel Meade, his voice betraying both shock and astonishment.

She removed the saw from the crack in the door. "Let me out."

But the bolt was already being drawn back and Meade stood upright and blessedly normal by the light of the lantern in his hold.

"Dear God, what has happened to you?" he exclaimed, as though involuntarily.

"Where is Lily?" she demanded.

"I don't know. I was looking for her when I found you. We were meant to meet on the terrace just before the supper dance, but she didn't come, and I didn't see her in the ballroom. The thing is, she didn't come out either..."

"Then she's still in the house," Tabitha said grimly, striding back along the path. "I should have known Ralph had tricked me twice over. We must find her immediately."

"I agree, but my lady, do you really want to be seen in the ballroom like that?"

"Like what?" she demanded impatiently.

"Your hands are bleeding all over your torn gloves. There's dirt on your face and your gown, and cobwebs in your hair."

Tabitha opened her mouth to deny that any of that mattered. Although, of course it did. She swerved toward the kitchen entrance.

"Besides," she muttered, "Chivers is the man we need. Nothing happens in this house without his knowledge."

There was no obstacle to their entry through the kitchen door. A whole gaggle of people were discovered in the servants' hall, enjoying a well-earned rest around the table. No doubt supper was all prepared and laid out in the ballroom's large ante-chamber, giving the servants the remainder of this dance—music could clearly be heard drifting over from the ballroom—before they would have to serve it.

At sight of Tabitha and Meade, they all leapt to their feet in varying degrees of horror and alarm. Chivers surged toward them.

"My stepdaughter is missing," Tabitha snapped at him. "Where is she?"

"Perfectly safe, my lady," Chivers soothed. "She is with the mistress."

"Where?" Tabitha demanded, although with marginally less fear.

But Chivers's eyes swivelled. "I am not at liberty to say, my lady."

"You will not be at liberty at all if you don't," Tabitha said savagely.

He looked positively frightened now. "But it is a wedding, my lady..."

"Without *me*?"

Chivers's eyes widened. He swallowed.

"You must speak," Meade said, every inch the army officer in command.

"I cannot imagine the mistress meant to exclude your ladyship."

"Where?" Tabitha demanded.

Chivers sagged. "The library, my lady. Let me show you in."

Neither Tabitha nor Meade waited to be shown. They flew up the servants' stairs and across the hallway to the closed library door. Meade turned the handle.

Suddenly, Tabitha was terrified what she would discover on the other side of the door.

"It's locked," Meade said.

"I'll fetch the key," Chivers said, and bolted.

Inside the room someone cried out. There were frightening, scuffling sounds and grunts and someone saying in an unnaturally high, pleading voice, "Isbourne! Jack! Jack, *please...*"

Of course he would never agree to this wedding, but what in God's name were they doing to him?

Tabitha raised both her fists to the door and thumped desperately once before Meade said curtly, "Stand back."

He didn't trouble with knocking, merely lifted his smart, military boot, and kicked viciously, twice.

The wood splintered and the door flew open.

Jack, his hair tangled and his coat ripped at the shoulder, was wrestling and heaving in the hold of Carily and Cousin Ralph. Close by, Lord Hazlett appeared to be wringing his hands. Louisa had covered her face in horror and Sir Peter, white faced, was commanding helplessly, "Stop this! Stop this now!"

At the sight of Tabitha, everyone froze, like a Hogarth drawing of some disreputable scene. Through it, Jack's wild, furious gaze clashed into Tabitha's.

As though he couldn't help it, his face broke into a blazing smile that stole her breath.

Carily, taking advantage of his captive's stillness, swung back his fist.

Meade strode forward, and grasped the fist, wrenching it hard behind Carily's back. "Unhand my friend," he snarled.

Jack, freed so abruptly on one side, backhanded Carily almost casually in the mouth while pulling free of Ralph. He strode straight to Tabitha, and she to him, grasping both his hands.

"Tabbie!" Lily cried, launching herself from Louisa's side. "What have they done to you?"

Tabitha spared her a long, searching glance and, finding her state satisfactory in the circumstances, returned to Jack. He had drawn her hands to his lips, softly kissing the cuts and blisters.

"She was locked in a garden shed," Meade said tightly, "and was sawing her way out when I found her."

But Ralph, it seemed, never knew when to give up. "The question is, why was she there? And who with? Entirely unsuitable! No wonder I am reduced to marrying my poor cousin out of hand to this kind and generous gentleman. It is all I can do to save her from this —"

"You will be quiet," Jack said, and stunningly, Ralph was.

"This has all gone horribly wrong," Lord Hazlett said, almost in a wail. "No one should be man-handling or hurting the duke. It is meant to be a wedding, not a prize fight. This was not what we discussed, Sark!"

"It was not what *we* discussed either, uncle," Jack said.

The agitated Hazlett dropped his gaze, but pleaded hoarsely, "Come away from that woman, Isbourne. She is not fit..."

"Fit," Jack repeated.

Wheatsheaf stepped forward, speaking with all the authority of his calling. "She is not. An immoral woman, fallen—"

"Immoral?" Jack stared at him so fiercely that the clergyman's words seemed to die in his throat. "Do you hear yourself? This lady has more integrity, more honesty in her little finger than anyone else in this room has ever shown!"

"Anyone except Nat," Lily said anxiously.

Jack's lips twitched. "Anyone except Nat. And our hosts, who I'm sure were tricked into supplying their respectable presence." His gaze refocused on Lord Hazlett. "You, I cannot forgive. Nor my former chaplain. In the circumstances—"

"*Former* chaplain?" cried Wheatsheaf, dismayed. "But your grace, it was all for you!"

This, Tabitha suspected, was where Jack usually gave in, accepting the apology and the apparent devotion. But the duke, it seemed, had learned much.

"Why should you imagine I want a chaplain who connives at imprisoning and hurting innocent women? At forcing a young girl into marriage against her will? Conspiring with an attempted murderer—oh yes, sir, I know all about your attempt to shoot the true Lord Sark. And I'm sure those documents spread so conveniently on the table there are your attempt to embezzle me out of a considerable amount of money under the guise of a wedding settlement for Lady Lily."

Everyone was silent now. Jack, maintaining a gentle hold on Tabitha's torn hands, held the floor completely.

"I believe, in the circumstances, Sir Peter and Lady Hawthorn, will forgive your early departure from this house. I'm sure their footmen will be ready to escort you from the premises—within five minutes at the most, for they have supper to serve and you have disrupted the household enough."

He returned his gaze to Tabitha and his eyes softened. "Come my love, let us see to your hurts. Lieutenant, please conduct Lady Lily to supper."

He placed Tabitha's hand on his arm and strolled out with a style that made Meade grin. Chivers, who had clearly if belatedly grasped the seriousness of the situation, had brought four burly footmen to oversee events.

"As his grace orders, Chivers," Sir Peter said, sounding slightly dazed but quite determined. "Discreetly, if you please."

FIFTEEN MINUTES LATER, Jack had bathed her hands. Allison had anointed them, brushed and sponged her gown clean, and was brushing out and restoring her hair to its former style.

"Some clean gloves, my lady, and no one will know. Are you sure you want to go back to the ball?"

"I want to dance with his grace," she said honestly.

Allison smiled. So did Jack, watching in the mirror as the maid reaffixed Tabitha's head-dress with jewel-headed pins.

"Your grace shouldn't be here," the maid pointed out as she straightened, finally satisfied.

"We'll go down in two minutes," Tabitha promised. "I need to see to Lily. But first, I have to speak to his grace."

Allison inclined her head and departed without fuss. In fact, she seemed to be smiling.

Tabitha turned to face Jack. "What will you do?"

"About my uncle? What I intended from the moment I spoke with my solicitor in London. He and the others have been taking liberties. Oh, not embezzling, simply fudging the truth a little. Full control of my person and my estate came to me on my twenty-first birthday. The Trust is no more, and my uncles have no authority. The trouble is, they liked it. I daresay there is affection and they tell themselves I am too sickly to cope, but I'm not and haven't been for some years. Much of the fault is mine because I accepted too much, was too unwilling to hurt the feelings of those I knew devoted their lives to me. But it goes no further. None of my uncles will be welcome in any of my properties until I receive a full apology in writing. Even then, the visits will be with fixed limits and solely on my terms."

"Good for you, Jack. I'm proud of you." She rose and went to perch on the arm of his chair. "No guilt attaches to you, you know. You acted—or failed to act—through kindness. That is a rare enough virtue in this world."

Another pair of white gloves sat on the opposite arm of the chair where Allison had left them. Jack picked them up and began to slip one over her fingers.

"I can't forgive any of them for what they did," he said quietly. "When I thought Ralph had hurt you, even killed you, I could not..."

She dropped her cheek onto their joined hands crushing the glove. "Neither could I. What are we going to do, Jack?"

He stroked her nape—about the only part of her he could touch without disturbing her hair or clothing. That made her smile too.

He said, "You could marry me. I know it's not what you want, but truly, all marriages are not like your first."

"I know. Is there an alternative?"

"I would gladly be your lover," he said softly. "It would make me the happiest of men and I count the privilege a gift beyond price."

She raised her head, gazing into his face. "You do?"

"I do. And yet I want more. I think I will always want more. I want to share everything with you—my name, my home, my children if we are so blessed, my whole life. And yours."

"Oh, Jack," she whispered, lowering her face to his, her lips parting.

It was a sweet kiss, lingering, tender, and full of promise.

"Will you think about it?" he asked huskily.

"I will." She rose with sudden briskness, pulling her other glove on and reaching for her reticule. "Shall we go into supper and make sure Lily is behaving?"

"We shall." He stood and winged his arm, and she laid her hand on his sleeve.

Together, they walked to the bedchamber door, yet when he reached to open it, she caught his hand and stared up at him.

Jack. Her wonderful, unique, Jack... When she had been so afraid of losing him...

She caught her breath. A world of forever was opening up in her mind, not with fear or horror or doubt, but with gleeful, wondrous anticipation. She could be happy. With *him*. She could *only* be happy with him.

"Oh, the devil, Jack," she said brokenly. "Just marry me! I—"

The rest was lost in his mouth as he kissed her with searing, desperate need.

And when, finally, he lifted his head, his breath somewhat ragged, they walked unhurriedly back to the ballroom together. She need never be afraid or lonely ever again. Quite suddenly life was blazing with gladness and promise.

The ESCAPE Series

Available now:

Escape of the Scoundrel

Escape of the Bridegroom

Escape of the Highwayman

Escape of the Duke

Coming soon:

Escape of the Duellist

About the Author

Mary Lancaster is a USA Today bestselling author of award-winning historical romance and other historical fiction. She lives in Scotland with her husband, one of three grown-up kids, and a small dog with a big personality.

Her first literary love was historical fiction, a genre which she relishes mixing up with romance and adventure in her own writing. Several of her novels feature actual historical characters as diverse as Hungarian revolutionaries, medieval English outlaws, and a family of eternally rebellious royal Scots. To say nothing of Vlad the Impaler.

More recently, she has enjoyed writing light, fun Regency romances, with occasional forays into historical mystery.

CONNECT WITH MARY ON-line – she loves to hear from readers:

Website: http://www.MaryLancaster.com

Newsletter sign-up: https://www.MaryLancaster.com/Newsletter

Facebook: https://www.facebook.com/mary.lancaster.1656

Facebook Author Page: https://www.facebook.com/MaryLancasterNovelist/

Amazon Author Page: https://www.amazon.com/Mary-Lancaster/e/B00DJ5IACI

Bookbub: https://www.bookbub.com/profile/mary-lancaster

X: @MaryLancNovels https://x.com/MaryLancNovels

Bluesky: @MaryLancaster.bsky.social

TikTok: https://www.tiktok.com/@mary.lancaster1

www.ingramcontent.com/pod-product-compliance
Lightning Source LLC
Chambersburg PA
CBHW020307150626
46552CB00022B/2061